JIM NASH

LOBO

PX DUKE

Jim Nash Read Order

JIM NASH

Jim Nash The Beginning
Pirate Cay
Thrill Kill Jill
Greetings From Key West
Lost Paradise
No Angels
Mexico Gamble
No Picnic
Fallen Angels
Vendetta
A Girl's Best Friend
Dead End
No Harbor
Dog Days
Startup Blues
Last Stop To Nowhere / The Last Goodbye
Revenge Is Justice
Escape
Wedding Bell Blues
Snap Brim Fedora Caper
Breakdown
Little Girl Lost
Forget Me Not
All The Glitter
Mexico Time
Partners In Crime
Shop Till You Drop
Lobo
No Free Ride
Gone
Stealing America
Blame It on Djibouti
No Escape
Trouble in Paradise
Nash & Delaney Collide

SEASONAL

Trick or Treat
Helping Santa

JIM NASH INVESTIGATES

The Snap Brim Fedora Caper
The Lady in White
The Lady in Yellow

Print books

Jim Nash

Jim Nash The Beginning
Gun Crazy
Gun Crazy 2
Gun Crazy 3
Fallen Angels
Last Stop to Nowhere
Revenge is Justice
Escape / Forget Me Not
Wedding Bell Blues / Breakdown
Mexico Time
No Free Ride / Gone
LOBO
Stealing America
Blame It on Djibouti
No Escape
Trouble in Paradise
Nash & Delaney Collide

Harry Delaney Adventures

Dead Reckoning
Lie Cheat Steal
Uncharted
Go-Around
Sand Storm
Harry Delaney Collection

Frank Ross Biker Tales

No Way Out
Bad Girls
Bank Robber Dames

Other

The Last President

JIM NASH

LOBO

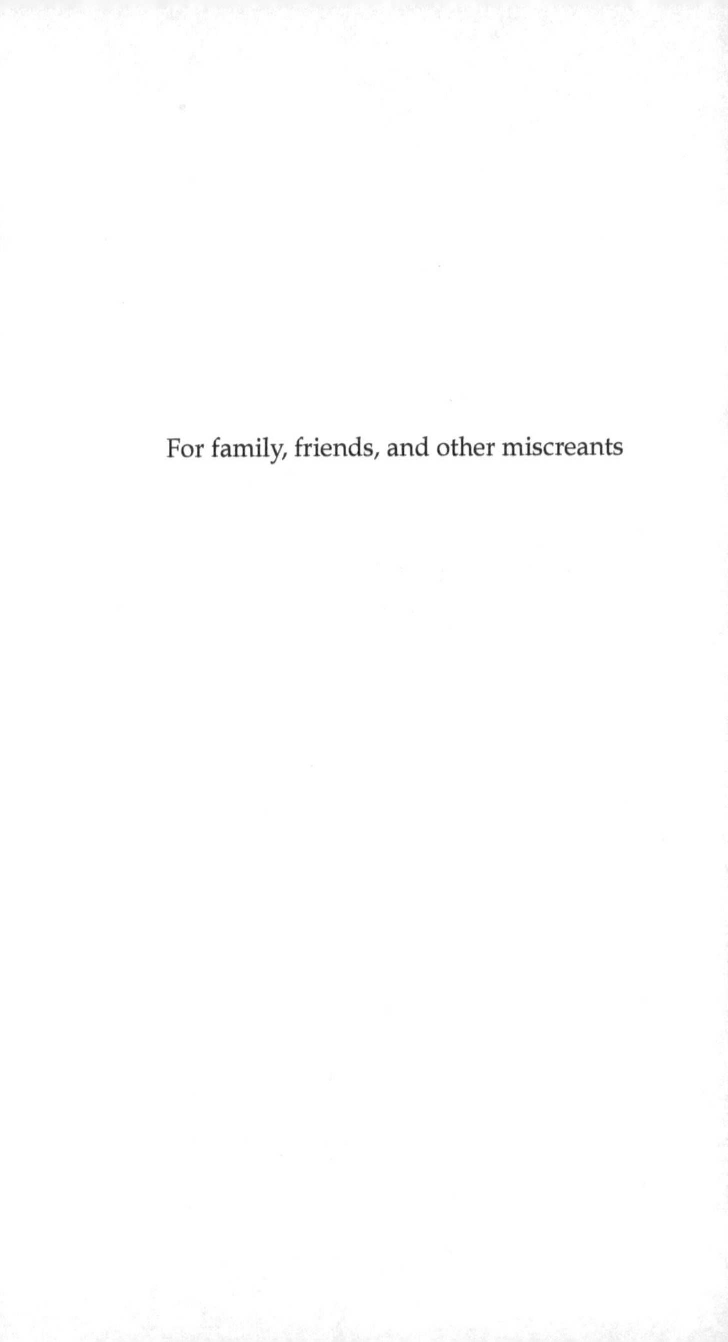

For family, friends, and other miscreants

The Mexican wolf, known as El Lobo, or more simply, Lobo, is facing extinction. The few remaining fight to survive.

Chapter 1

J im Nash held open the downstairs door and allowed Friday and Lola to scramble into the building ahead of him. He unhooked their leashes and, side by side, the dogs leaped up the stairs.

They halted briefly on the first-floor landing, did some loud sniffing, and bolted to the closed office door. They paused only long enough to sniff and snort. Disappointed, they rushed up the stairs to the third floor, where they separated.

Lola, the yellow Lab, plopped her rear-end down on the floor. Her tail swished back and forth as she waited, impatient. Friday, the black Lab, tore down the hallway. He halted briefly at the two apartment doors before hurrying back to Lola's side.

Jim opened the office door and saw the note on his desk. He read it and then replaced it on his office desk. He trudged up the stairs after Lola and Friday to the third-floor apartment he shared with Maddie Spence and the dogs. By the time he caught up, they were in a frenzy to get past the closed door.

Jim wasn't in a hurry. He already knew Maddie wasn't there to greet them. The dogs didn't know that. He slipped the key in the door and pushed it open.

Four pairs of furry legs beat him to it. Tails wagged in anticipation. Heads lowered. Noses swept the floor. Heads moved back and forth. Directions changed abruptly as they scampered from room to room in the large apartment. Unsuccessful in their quest, they returned. Furry bottoms plopped down at Jim's feet. Two pairs of mournful dark brown eyes looked up.

"I'm sorry, boys and girls, but Maddie isn't here."

The dogs cocked their heads on hearing Maddie's name. Ears perked up.

"She's run off to the Keys for some time away. At least, that's what the note says. What do you say we go check on the other two?" He tramped down the hall to Anya's. Read the yellow note stuck to it.

Gone with Maddie. Back in a few.

He ambled down to Emma Mayberry's apartment. Another note said basically the same thing.

"Well, dogs, it looks like we've been left to our own devices. What do you say we celebrate with a bit of a snooze before lunch?" He looked around and realized he was talking to himself. He made his way to the bedroom. The dogs were waiting.

"You two better not let Maddie see you up on our bed. There'll be hell to pay for all three of us."

Friday looked guilty. Lola stretched out on Maddie's side of the bed.

Jim reached down to scratch behind two pairs of furry ears and that seemed to placate the dogs, at least for the time being. He settled on the bed and the dogs rearranged themselves to give him room.

He didn't fall asleep right away. He worried about Maddie, although not so much this time. When she worked a case, she was always alone, unless, of course, he was backing her up. This time, she was on a well-deserved break with Emma and Anya. What trouble could she get into with those two?

He fell into restful sleep before he could answer that one.

Somewhere in the apartment, Jim's cell phone rang. He looked across the bed at the dogs, still fast asleep. Obviously, they weren't interested in disturbing themselves to answer it. He stumbled out of the bedroom, found the phone, and mumbled into it. Whoever was on the other end wasn't sure.

"Jim? Is that you? It's Don."

In his sleepy state of mind, Jim almost didn't recognize Don. "What? Don. Yeah. How have you been? Long time no see."

"I can tell Maddie isn't there or you wouldn't be fast asleep in the middle of the day."

"Yeah, she and the neighbors are out on a girl weekend thing. Apparently, they've been planning it for a while. I'm babysitting the dogs. We just got back from a run and the dogs needed rest. What's up?" Jim already knew Don wouldn't be falling for that story, and he was right.

"Uh-huh. Next thing you know, you'll have a house full of kids. I've got some time off coming up. I was wondering if you want to desert civilization as we know it and go fishing for a few days."

Jim laughed. Don Boyle was a Lieutenant in Magic City's PD. He met him while working a case a few years ago and they got along. Don convinced him to get his PI license. He had helped shepherd his application through the system.

"Did you clear it with the wife first?" he asked.

Don's wife Nancy and daughter Tricia were favorites of Maddie and of him, too. Not to mention Friday's tea parties with Trish.

Don mumbled a Yes, I got the okay, and Jim instantly felt guilty for teasing the man.

"Don't mind me. I'm stuck with two dogs for a day. Not complaining, just saying. I don't think I'd like to take both of them away with us. Lola is still an inquisitive puppy, and she's a handful with Friday to lead her astray. Do you think—"

Don didn't hesitate. "Already discussed with wifey. Nancy and Tricia will be happy to take Friday and Lola off your hands for two or three days."

Jim didn't waste time with his reply. "I'll let

her take Friday. I think Lola would be a bit of a handful, even for Trish, although I'm sure she'd like to have an overgrown puppy over for tea. You've got a deal," he said. "If you don't mind Lola coming along for the ride."

It would be good for Lola to get out and about and socialize. The more Jim thought about it, the more he liked the idea. "As long as you don't mind having a dog that's trained by Friday and only sometimes by me."

"Sounds like she's a handful," Don said and laughed. "I'm reminded of someone else in your household.

Jim laughed with him. "Yeah, you got me there. Welcome to my world. I'll see you in a bit, okay?"

J im packed up dog food and toys and bowls for two dogs and managed to think of himself with a bag, too. For luck, he tossed his Model 17 automatic in the bag with a couple of oversize magazines and two boxes of shells. The five-shot backup went into the bag, too, complete with ankle holster.

Better to not need it and have it than the other way around.

Immediately he felt sheepish. It was a fishing trip, after all.

He made three trips down the stairs to the car and loaded the trunk with Friday's and Lola's belongings. He looked in to check the goods before shaking his head and closing the trunk.

Just like having kids.

Jim was about to get in the car when he remembered the dogs and his own bag. He rushed up the stairs and leashed Lola. He didn't want her wandering off, even if Friday would happily run herd on her.

"Come on, boys and girls. Road trip."

Friday knew the words. Lola was still in learning mode. She didn't have more than a car trip or two to remember. Friday led the way and barked out his shotgun. Lola jumped into the back, and Friday changed his mind and did the same.

"Make up your mind or I'll leave you at home, dog." He wasn't serious, of course. Still, if Maddie was here, he'd get a dirty look. He smiled and waited for the dogs to settle in. No sooner was he behind the wheel than Friday brushed his neck with a cold, wet nose. Lola took her cue and did the same.

"Zelda. I mean Friday. Bad dog. Lola, you're a bad dog, too."

Friday didn't listen. He did it again. Lola did it, too, throwing in a wet lick just for spite. He laughed and reached back to pet the pair of them.

"All right, you two. Let the road trip begin."

Jim turned the old Packard into the Boyle driveway. Already Friday was antsy to get out. Lola wasn't so sure. She looked from Jim to Friday. "It's okay, girl. Tricia wants to meet you."

Friday bounded up the steps to greet the girl.

Tricia grinned like she wouldn't quit, and when Lola nuzzled her hand with a wet nose, she giggled. "Is Lola staying too, Uncle Jim?" the girl wanted to know.

He didn't want to disappoint the girl. He had no choice. "She's just a puppy, Tricia. She needs a lot of socializing. I convinced your dad to let me bring Lola along. Do you think you'll be all right with Friday all by himself?"

Tricia's mother, Nancy, regarded Jim with a smile. "When did you become such a diplomat, James Nash?"

He blushed and changed the subject when he saw Tricia sitting on the step with a dog on each side. Her arms circled the necks of both dogs.

"Look at that. I'm sorely tempted."

Nancy smiled down at her daughter. "Well don't be, James. I have a proposition for you. Our fee is your car. Leave it with us for the duration and we'll be happy."

"Mrs. Boyle, you've got yourself a deal."

Jim unloaded the trunk and carefully placed the goods into two piles, one for Friday, and the other for Lola. He carted Friday's food and gear into the house. Tricia helped and soon there was only Lola's things and his bag and fishing kit remaining on the driveway.

He slammed the trunk and handed the keys to Nancy. "Thank you, Nance. Maddie is off with our neighbors on a break and I was going stir-crazy with two dogs to look after."

"It's not a problem. I enjoy having Friday over. Tricia loves him. He's almost as well-behaved as you are." She laughed and shooed everyone into the house. "I made sandwiches for two days and threw in a store-bought baked chicken and all the fixings. If you come back complaining about being hungry, you're out of luck."

Tricia opened the fridge and took out a package. "I made cookies for you and dad, Uncle Jim."

"In that case, I can't wait, young lady. The pair of you are enough to make a man want to get married."

Nancy laughed again.

Tricia blushed.

"If Maddie was here, I don't think you'd be saying that."

Nancy was forever teasing the pair about getting hitched.

He knew she was only half serious. He would never admit that it made him more than a bit nervous.

Don arrived, and they jockeyed the cars and began loading the trunk. "I've arranged for an RV rental at our campsite," said. "No tenting for real men, Nash."

With the car loaded, Don waved at Nancy and Trish. Friday woofed and wagged his tail. The last thing Jim heard was Tricia inviting Friday up the stairs for story time in her room.

Lola nudged Don's neck with her wet nose.

Jim saw her. "Lola. Bad dog," he told her. "Don't bother the driver."

Don reached back from the driver's seat to scratch at Lola's ears. His wide smile belied Jim's gruff tone.

"Don't mind her. She picked up most of Friday's bad habits and a few of mine, too," Jim said.

Lola nosed Don's neck again before settling in the back seat and sticking her head out the window.

"What was that about a camper?" Jim wanted to know. "Just how much is all the fish we catch going to cost me, Boyle?"

"You get half the fish and half the bill, my friend. Just like always," Don said.

Chapter 2

Don **parked the car** and went in to the small office to register for the RV and the campsite.

Lola stood up in the back seat and whined, waiting for the man's return. The reaction to an absent Don surprised Jim. "Don't worry, girl. Your new bestie will be back in a minute."

Lola's tail did double-time when Don showed himself and made for the car. He took his seat behind the wheel and the dog's cold, wet nose went through the nudging routine all over again.

"Nancy better not find out there's a new woman in my life. Tricia either. They'll never forgive me."

Don steered for the camping spot and the RV squatting on it.

Jim said, "We'll never tell, will we, Lola? Let me get her leash. I don't want her running off to investigate her new surroundings in an RV park filled with strangers."

Jim got out and screwed an anchor stake into the firm, sandy ground beneath the shade of the RV's awning. He unloaded Lola's water bowl and filled it before setting it down. He hooked the long leash to the stake, and the dog busied herself lapping up the bottled water. Satisfied, she headed off to test the bounds of her new surroundings.

Don couldn't resist the wisecrack. "It appears to me you're familiar with the old ball and chain routine. Maddie would be pleased if she found out." He went on before Jim could respond. "Did you notice that old-school diner by the turnoff? I'm going to pick up some coffee. Are you good to load up the fridge with wifey's contributions to our waistlines?"

Jim didn't need to be asked twice. He was more than familiar with Nancy's provisioning. "No sweat, partner. I'll have the fridge packed and dessert ready."

He busied himself unloading the coolers from the trunk while Don took Lola for a short walk.

Jim wondered what Nancy had waiting for them. She always made it a point to prepare something sweet for them to work on at the end of a fishing day.

And there were Tricia's cookies, too.

The sun was setting beneath an orange horizon by the time Don made for the diner and the almost-empty parking lot. He hoped it was only closing time and not because of the food. He pushed open the door. A loud cow bell hanging from the door frame clanged to announce his arrival. The bell clanged again when the door closed.

Several pairs of eyes gave him the once-over.

He proceeded to an empty stool at the far end of the counter where he could monitor the half-empty room out of habit. He kept busy waiting for service by watching customers studying their bills while reaching for wallets.

"What's your pleasure, boss? If you want to eat, you're out of luck. We'll be closing shortly."

Don looked up. Studied the server in front of him like any man checking out an attractive woman while trying not to be obvious.

A deadpan face looked down at him.

"You gotta be quick, mister." The server chomped on gum between sentences. "The grill is off. The place is emptying, and I need to cash out and count my tips. We're shorthanded tonight."

He ordered two large to go. "Cream and sugar, please."

"Two? You out with your wife, are ya?" There was more gum-chewing.

Don gestured to the window. "We're camped across the highway. I've got an RV for three or four days. Doing the fishing thing with a buddy. What time do you open in the morning?"

"We open at five. See you then."

The server returned with the goods. She made sure to place the bill in the flat of her hand with a practiced motion before slapping it on the counter. Don ignored the proffered bill and picked up the two coffees.

"Don't you want the bill, mister?"

"Not necessary. Here's your tip." He slid some coins across the counter.

The woman placed her hand over the bill and slid it toward him. "You'll need this, I'm pretty sure."

He gave the server a strange look before picking it up. He ignored the bill and folded it before putting it in his shirt pocket.

It was no big deal. When he and Jim went on their fishing trips, they shared expenses to the dollar.

They tallied up the receipts when they got home.

Chapter 3

Nancy **Boyle looked out** the front window and took in Jim's beautifully restored 1956 Packard convertible sitting in the driveway. The dark maroon and off-white color scheme appeared rather mysterious. She thought for a moment before finally calling to her daughter. Friday traipsed after the little girl because he was a nosy dog, and he didn't spend as much time as he liked with these two females.

"Dear, what say we take Uncle Jim's car for a drive?"

Friday recognized the words—they almost sounded like car ride—and barked.

Tricia jumped up and down with glee. "Can we put the top down?"

"Of course we can. Let's get ready. You take Friday for a quick walk and I'll find something for us to wear."

Tricia called to the dog. "Walk, Friday. Time for a walk to do your business."

The words sounded nothing like what he was expecting, but it was better than nothing. Friday retrieved his leash and dropped it at

Tricia's feet. She attached it, and the pair stepped outside.

Nancy paused and thought for a minute before heading upstairs to the bedroom. She changed her mind and proceeded to the basement door. She opened it and flipped on the light to make her way downstairs to a storage room.

She flipped on another light to illuminate an old trunk stowed in a corner. It hadn't been opened in ages, as evidenced by the dust covering it. She found a rag and carefully dusted the top before undoing the catches and flipping it open.

She rummaged through the ancient trunk's interior, shifting contents and sliding smaller boxes to reveal more boxes. She held up several articles of clothing that once belonged to her mother, and a few more that her grandmother had worn.

She settled on three silk scarves. She held them to her nose and inhaled the familiar perfume.

These will have to do for now.

She looked through a small cardboard box and found several pairs of old sunglasses. She selected a vintage pair of cat-eyes and another of glitter bubbles before returning the boxes and closing the trunk.

She returned upstairs to look through her bedroom closet but wasn't able to find anything that suited her fancy. She didn't bother going into Tricia's room.

She took the scarves to the dryer and threw

them in on a fluff cycle.

While she waited for Tricia and the dog to return, she remembered another old box in the bedroom. It was on a top shelf. She was about to open it when she heard Tricia calling out.

"Friday piddled, mom. We can go now."

Nancy made for the dryer to retrieve the scarves. "I have something for us to try on until we get downtown. Come and check it out."

Tricia made for the laundry room. The dog scurried after her with feet slipping on the tile floor.

"Follow me to the hall mirror, boys and girls," Nancy called out.

Friday woofed, pleased with himself that he noticed the happy females and their sunglasses and scarves.

Nancy looped a scarf around his neck and tied it off.

He preened, pleased to be the center of attention with his very own scarf.

"Here we go. We look perfect for the age of Uncle Jim's car. Once we get to where we're going, the look will get even better."

It wasn't Nancy's first go-round with a convertible. Her husband, Don, had courted her in one. Still, she had to look for the release handles. She cursed silently when she broke a nail, but ended up with a broad smile when the electric motor hummed and the top went down.

"Front or back, Friday?"

Trish opened the passenger door and pulled the seat-back forward for the dog.

He jumped in and took up his usual position behind the driver's seat.

Nancy leaned in and adjusted Friday's scarf. His tail wagged as best it could against the back of the seat as his tongue slurped her hand.

Tricia giggled at her mom's and the dog's antics.

"Where are we going, Mommy? Somewhere special?"

"You'll see when we get there, dear. For now, just enjoy the atmosphere."

Nancy turned the key in the ignition. The old Packard roared to life. Her eyes roamed the interior. "Look at this, Tricia."

She caressed the expanse of bench seat between them.

"That's real leather. And thick carpet on the floor, not the cheap stuff we get now. This is a real beauty. Uncle Jim must be very proud of it."

She turned on the satellite radio receiver and tuned in a 1940s music station. Frank Sinatra crooned over the airwaves.

She didn't have to wrestle with the gearshift. It slipped easily into reverse. She backed the car onto the street, straightened, and shifted into drive.

Her foot barely touched the gas pedal. Tires squealed. The instant life in the old car surprised her.

"My goodness, but Uncle Jim did a lot of work on this beauty. It steers like a dream. The brakes are excellent. And it even has air."

Friday placed a cold nose on the back of

Nancy's neck. She giggled like a schoolgirl.

Tricia looked across at her mom. "Friday likes you."

She reached back to scratch at the dog, but already he was settled in the seat, out of reach. He sat like an emperor on parade, taking in the sights with mouth open and tongue hanging out as the top-down breeze caressed his face.

Nancy ignored the waves from the other drivers and the honking horns.

Tricia wasn't so shy. She grinned and waved and enjoyed the attention.

Friday did too, as evidenced by the occasional bark.

"Here we are, dear."

Nancy eased the car into the parking spot in front of the store.

"Wait here a moment. I'll be right back."

Chapter 4

Jim busied himself going through his tackle box while he waited for Don and the coffee. It had been ages since his last fishing trip with Don, and the box needed work. He began by sorting his lures, untangling as he went. He carried on a one-sided conversation with Lola at the same time.

The dog kept one ear cocked slowly wagged a tail in response.

Don drew closer to hear Jim humming an old song, and he paused to listen. When the man got to the refrain, he sang out the dog's name, L-o-l-a, Lola. The tan Labrador's ears went erect, and she cocked her head before nosing Jim's thigh.

Her reward was an ear scratch.

Lola looked up at Jim.

Don smiled at the dog's antics. He slid the coffee across the table. Jim closed the lid on the tackle box. "Did you and Lola get everything organized for tomorrow morning?" he asked.

Lola sidled up to Don, nosed his thigh, and appeared satisfied at the reaction she got when the man reached to scratch behind an ear.

She returned to Jim's side and settled in.

"She's a fickle thing, isn't she?"

Don considered what he had witnessed in the diner. He decided on the spot the indirect route would solve what he had witnessed.

"Didn't you say Maddie and the girls were on a getaway somewhere? Where did you say they were going again?" he asked.

"They're on the Keys somewhere," Jim said. "I'm not sure where. I don't expect we'll run into them. They aren't into fishing. At least, I don't think they are."

Don considered for a moment before sliding the receipt across the table.

Jim looked at him. "Are we splitting right off? Usually, we wait till the end."

"Take a look, James."

Jim grabbed the receipt and fished in his pocket for his wallet.

"Don't pay me yet. Look on the back. What does it say? I can't make it out. Luze. Or something. I don't know what it is."

Jim flipped the paper over. He recognized the name immediately. And Maddie's writing.

Startled, his elbow bumped the unlatched tackle box. It slid off the table and crashed to the ground, spilling the contents.

"It's pronounced *Loos*. It's a girl's name. Luz. When did Maddie give it to you?"

Jim didn't see Lola moving to investigate the strange mess in the sand.

Don called to the dog. "Come, Lola. You don't want to be sticking your cold, wet nose into your master's tackle box. Or a paw. Come sit by me." He patted his thigh.

Jim couldn't recall talking about Luz with Maddie more than once or twice.

"You didn't tell me when she gave it to you."

He flipped the receipt over and tried to read the date.

"About ten minutes ago." It was all Don said.

Jim didn't believe what he was hearing. "From Maddie? No way." He turned to look at the diner behind him.

Don regarded his friend. His immediate thought was Jim brought him down here while the pair were working a case. Except, he was the one to make the invitation. "Is Maddie working a job?"

Jim looked exasperated. "Hell no, Don. She's supposed to be taking some time off. I think the three of us were getting to her, so she rounded up the neighbors and took off on a trip."

Surely the women hadn't gone off on their own on a job without telling him. Had they?

"Yeah, well, she was chewing gum and slinging hash gum in that diner. I didn't see the other two, but by the time I noticed, they could have checked out. Where do you think you're going?"

Jim was up and making for the street.

"Get back here, Nash. You don't know what she's doing. And you sure don't want to blow anything she's working on, whether she told you or didn't."

Jim sighed and sat down. Don was right.

He called to Lola. The dog trotted over and sat at his feet. He scratched absentmindedly at her ears and she let loose with her own sigh.

"I already know your plan, Nash. You're going to walk the dog to see if she picks up Maddie's scent. Not a good idea. Besides, you would have recognized her car if she was in the campground."

Don was right. He had already walked the dog through the campsite while Don was at the diner. Other than the usual smell-all-the-smells rambling Lola did, there was nothing that pointed the dog anywhere in particular.

"Maddie mentioned the place opens at five in the morning. Are you good till then?"

"I guess I'm going to have to be."

Don went into the RV and returned with drinks and a plate of Nancy's sandwiches. He allowed Jim to think while he refreshed Lola's water and filled her food bowl. He set it on the ground and Lola greeted him like a long-lost friend. "I think she likes me so far."

"She would. You're feeding her. Even Friday likes me then, too. What the hell is that woman doing here?"

"You might as well stop thinking about it. You won't know anything until tomorrow, if then. Tell me about the name on the receipt."

It was a chance to get Jim thinking about something else. It worked when Nash took it instead of rushing off to search for Maddie.

Chapter 5

Jim Nash settled in, resigned to telling Don Boyle about Luz and her involvement in the shootout he had found himself in.

"It's a long story. I'll give you the short version." He bit into a sandwich and washed it down with a swig of beer. Fishing with Don was the only time he allowed himself the pleasure.

"Did you see the news reports of the firefight on the wharf in Cabo?" he asked.

"I watched it like everyone else. You must be KOS down there by now."

"Kill on sight. I never thought about it like that, but yeah, you're probably right. Some of those people are long on memory and short on forgiveness for sure."

How much should he tell Don? Part of it? The entire story? He decided it had to be the action on the wharf. That was where Luz saved his bacon. Anya's, too.

"Do you remember the person behind us? The one covering us off? She was a ways behind, farther down the wharf."

Don nodded. "I do. That was a woman?

Hell, she was a real pro at advancing on whoever was flinging the lead at you. Nothing was going to stop that one."

The shooter in the video had been wearing a mask and was unrecognizable.

"She kept on coming like someone bent on revenge for sure," Don said.

Jim hesitated, thinking back to that day before going on. "That was Luz. I owe her everything." He couldn't deny it. Why would he?

"Holy shit, Nash. She really knew how to lay down fire with that AK. She looked like a regular in an action movie."

"Anya was with me. The shooter saved her bacon for sure," Jim said. "But it was Luz who saved all of us. She was only a girl. Fourteen or fifteen, tops."

Don gasped. "What? That's only a few years older than Trish.

Jim halted. He pulled the note out of his pocket and turned it over. Luz. What was up with Luz? Maddie only knew about her from what he told her about the Baja deal. He hadn't wanted to share much with her.

"That country—" he began.

Don said, "Messed up with drugs, thanks to this country. Is it possible Looze is trying to get out? To get here?"

"It's pronounced Luz, like in loose."

Jim considered before answering.

"Anything is possible. I do know Anya and Luz promised to stay in touch. Maybe they talked or did the texting thing. Maybe Luz is here now." Jim halted, thinking.

Could it be?

"Yeah, that has to be it. I wonder if Reynaldo is here, too."

"Reynaldo?"

"Her cousin. He was on the wharf that day, too. He was her lookout, tasked to keep an eye on us when we arrived in the fast-boat. Then Luz showed up to finish the deal. I thought I left her by Todos. She was the one that got us the go-fast we tied up at the Cabo wharf.

"Todos?"

"Todos Santos. On the west side of Baja sur. Roughly half-way between La Paz and Cabo. That country. Cartel kingpins and their drugs are killing it and everything in it."

Jim stood up. He had enough of the reminiscing. Enough wondering why Maddie hadn't told him about Luz. If that was indeed what was going on. "I'm going to hit the sack."

"Do I need to lock us in, Nash?"

Don called to Lola.

"No," he insisted. "I'm not going to blow anyone's cover. If it concerns Luz, I owe her everything, like I said. Did you bring a sidearm?"

"Both of them. Clean up your tackle box mess while I take your dog for her walk. Come on, Lola."

Don stood up and patted his thigh. Lola trotted up to him.

"Have you got her chew toy to give her a break?" Jim asked.

"Of course." Don pulled his shirt aside,

revealing his sidearm.

Jim raised an eyebrow and grinned. "Are you going to shoot her if she misbehaves? Tricia won't be too happy with the likes of you."

"Whoops. Wrong side." Don grinned and pulled open the other side of his shirt to reveal Lola's chew toy tucked into his belt.

Jim guessed Lola wasn't Don's first dog.

Before he could ask, Don and Lola disappeared into the campground's quiet nighttime.

Chapter 6

Nancy Boyle made her way into the Retro Owl on her way to the till. She passed several racks of clothing on the way. She halted at the cashier and the young sales clerk wearing a name tag that said Melanie. "I'm wondering if I can bring my dog in. He's very well-behaved, I promise."

The clerk had already noticed the car pulling to a halt in front of the store. Experience told her the customers would be up to something, given that she knew the car was old. "Of course you can. That's a beautiful vintage car."

"Thank you, Melanie. We think so, too."

Nancy returned to the door and called to Tricia and the dog. "It's all right, dear. You can bring Friday. He's allowed to help us shop."

Tricia walked Friday up to the clerk and introduced Friday.

Melanie made a fuss over the black dog, and a satisfied Friday traipsed off with the females. Nancy and Trish, accompanied by Melanie, cruised aisle after aisle of items in the vintage clothing section. Nancy told Melanie about the car. That it was vintage, from the mid-50s.

The clerk didn't need to hear more than that. She led them to the back of the store. "All our really vintage items are on these two racks. We don't have a lot, but what we have is very period-specific." Melanie gestured to the back wall. "We have hats and scarves over there in case you didn't notice."

Hangars rattled as Nancy began going through the vintage clothing. She picked several outfits and threw them over the rack to try on. One was a navy pin-dot swing dress with classic white crossover straps. Another was a classic off-the-shoulders evening gown.

Nancy moved to the rear wall and stood back to examine the items hanging on it. She picked a pair of vintage evening gloves and a couple of hats. One was a cute ivory downturn sun hat. For Tricia, she chose a black beret. She then selected a black bow mushroom hat. Finally, she picked out a couple of plaid spring scarves. "That should do it. What did you come up with, dear?"

Tricia showed her mom a pair of black and white saddle shoes. She held up a blue poodle skirt. "Do you think Friday will mind?"

"Oh no, dear. He'll love it. Let's find you a couple of blouses to go with that skirt."

Nancy made for the till to show the clerk their choices. "Would you mind keeping Friday for us while we try these on?"

Melanie was delighted. The dog flirted with her. Nosed her hand. Nudged her leg. Wagged his tail and looked up with big brown eyes.

"Can I feed him some chicken tenders from my lunch?"

"Of course. Tiny bites only," Nancy insisted.

Friday sat down at the end of the counter. His happy tail swept the floor when the female fed him a small bite of chicken.

Nancy and Tricia retreated to the change rooms where they busied themselves trying on their outfits.

A content Friday was already settled in with Melanie.

The counter concealed her every time she bent to give him treats and a pet.

Friday's gaze took in the male walking into the store. He recognized the object in the man's hand and emitted a low growl. He tensed. Got up on all fours.

Melanie gasped, startled by the dog's sudden change in demeanor from pet to threat.

Friday prepared to attack.

The frightened clerk sat back on her heels behind the counter. She still wasn't aware of the threat. She turned and crawled away from the dog on all fours.

Friday emitted a low growl. The surprised man expected to see a clerk behind the counter. He saw nothing and only heard a dog. Confused, he looked around. Didn't see anyone. Continued to walk toward the counter and the cash register with arm outstretched.

Friday launched in the man's direction.

A hundred-and-ten pounds of dog flew through the air. The clerk peeked around the edge of the counter in time to see the dog connect with the man's chest.

The handgun exploded.

The shot went wild.

The man fell backwards.

The huge black dog landed with a thump against the man's chest.

Man and dog crashed to the floor.

Friday moved off the stranger and crouched. His jaws locked on the arm that held the handgun.

The thief cried out and released the gun. It fell to the floor by the robber's head.

In the change room, Nancy heard the gunshot and the commotion. She forced Tricia to the floor before fishing in her handbag for the LC9 and a spare magazine.

"Honey. Stay down until I come for you, all right? I won't be long. I promise."

Tricia could only manage a nod.

"I know. You're scared. I'll only be a minute. I'll send Friday back to stay with you, okay?"

Tricia nodded.

Nancy held the Ruger at her thigh. The folds of the vintage dress concealed it. Her other hand was filled with the spare magazine. It, too, was hidden in the skirt.

She eased open the change room door.

Looked back at Tricia.

She smiled and nodded before silently making her way down the short hallway to look around the corner to the counter.

She spied Friday's rear end hunched down.

Recognized that every muscle was taut. His tail was straight up. She called to the dog. "Friday. Are you all right?"

The dog's growling ceased, and she began moving toward him.

He barked.

Someone groaned.

Friday growled, and the groans ceased.

Nancy called Melanie's name. "Where are you? Are you all right?"

"I think so. I'm not bleeding."

She recognized the clerk's voice coming from behind the counter. "Stay where you are, please. I have a gun."

Nancy approached the downed robber.

She called Friday to heel.

The dog backed up and remained by her side, still on alert, still tense.

She kicked the handgun away and bent to retrieve it.

She flipped open the cylinder and two live rounds fell into her hand. "He couldn't afford six. Shame."

She squatted beside the dog. "Good boy, Friday. Very good boy." She slapped his side, hard. The dog didn't relax for an instant.

"Melanie? Do you think you can sit on this guy while I call for backup?" she asked.

The clerk was no slouch. She rushed to grab a stiletto shoe from the rear wall and hurried back. She jumped on the still-groggy man's back and whacked him on the head with the sharp end.

He groaned.

Friday growled.

"Good boy, Friday. Good boy." Satisfied Melanie had things in hand, Nancy sent the dog off. "Find Tricia. Go find Tricia."

The dog relaxed immediately and scampered off, nose to ground, in the direction of the change room.

Tricia called to Friday and Nancy pictured her with her arms around the black Labrador. No doubt his tail would be flailing. She called to her daughter. "I'll be there in a minute, honey. Stay with Friday. Everyone out here is safe."

She turned to address Melanie, still sitting on the thief's back. Every time he moved, she bought the stiletto up with both hands and whacked him on the head.

"I'm going to leave some cash on the counter to pay our bill before we go, if that's all right. I'll call it in, and then I'm going to collect my daughter and our dog and we're going to leave. It looks to me like you can handle this guy by yourself."

She dialed 9-1-1 and called in the 10-29 and the 10-30, robbery and shooting.

The robber groaned again, and Nancy witnessed Melanie's response when she smashed the shoe into the back of his head with a vengeance.

"Listen to me, Melanie," she said. "When the police arrive, drop the shoe and raise your hands over your head. Understand?"

Melanie nodded.

"I need you to tell me you understand, dear."

Melanie nodded again. "I understand. Drop the shoe and raise my hands over my head."

"Good. We're off."

Sirens sounded in the distance.

"Here they come. You'll be just fine."

Nancy called to her partners in crime.

"Let's go, boys and girls. It's time we were out of here. We don't want Don to think we're a bunch of bad-asses."

Friday trotted up to the pair on the floor. He lowered his head to the thief and let go with a ferocious growl.

Melanie used it as an excuse to whack the man's head a final time.

"Move and I'll unleash the dog on you. Goodbye, Friday. Thank you. Happy days."

Nancy adjusted her sunglasses. Tricia, mimicking her mom, did the same.

Friday pranced up to the car door and waited patiently for his helpers.

Tricia opened the door, and he leaped into the back.

Nancy leaned in to adjust his classy neck scarf.

"You are a very good boy, Friday. Thank you for helping us."

She turned on the headlights and signaled the car into the street.

Police cars arrived behind her.

She glanced in the rearview to witness officers entering the store with weapons drawn.

"I hope Melanie does what I told her to do."

"She will, Mommy. Don't worry."

Nancy pulled onto the neon-lit strip. It was dark. Still early. She cruised it twice before pulling into an old-time ice cream store. A long counter and booths against the windows beckoned. She went in to ask if they could bring Friday in. She was rewarded with a yes and was told doggie ice cream was available to boot.

"Ice cream, Friday. A reward for a good boy."

Friday recognized those words instantly. He jumped out of the car and scampered into the store after the females. He ended up being served first when the server brought him a small bowl. He finished and looked up with huge brown eyes, an ice cream mustache and a cold, white nose.

"Oh Friday, you are such a cutie." Tricia reached down and hugged the dog. Her reward was a cold nose against her neck. She giggled.

It was all the reward the dog needed. Friday nuzzled her again, just because he could.

Chapter 7

Jim Nash tossed and turned in the close, humid quarters of the camper. He checked the clock. Turned his back to it. Tried to ignore it. When he looked again, it was past midnight. The ocean surf splashed. Curtains fluttered in the light breeze. He threw off the sheets, and it was a new hour before he finally admitted defeat.

He climbed out of bed and put the coffee pot on in the camper's tiny kitchen. He checked on Lola, fast asleep in her new surroundings. Satisfied and knowing coffee would soon be ready, he made for the picnic table to wait it out.

The RV door closed quietly behind him and Don stepped out.

"You checking up on me?" Jim asked.

"No. I couldn't sleep either. I was thinking about what you told me about that girl, Luz." Don got the pronunciation right. "I was wondering if perhaps Maddie is helping Anya to get her north into the country."

"Don't forget Emma is with them. Did you get to meet her? I don't remember."

Don pretended to think for a bit before replying. He well remembered when he first suspected Emma was the woman dressed in black and white accompanied by a huge black dog. He had a strong suspicion both were involved in a burning armored vehicle.

"I believe I did when you were laid up in the hospital recovering from that gunshot wound you took in Mexico. I didn't realize it, but I think Emma was the woman with the black dog who got rid of a van. Didn't she set fire to it or something?"

"No idea, Don. Like you said, I was laid up in the hospital. Not to mention, loose lips sink ships." Jim smiled.

Don stopped asking. He'd be retired before Jim told that story, especially since it had occurred on his watch in the department.

He changed the subject. "So, what's the plan for tomorrow, Nash?"

"I think I can kiss fishing goodbye until I know what those three are up to."

Don pushed back from the picnic table and stood up.

"You're not planning on leaving me out in the cold, are you? I want to know, too."

Chapter 8

Five a.m. didn't arrive soon enough for the men. They rushed to dress. Pistols slipped from holsters and magazines slid out and clicked back into automatic handguns. Both men found a measure of satisfaction in the sounds.

Don handed Jim a Hawaiian shirt.

"You better put this on. I can see the outline of your sidearm."

Jim held up the neatly pressed, colorful shirt and checked it out before unbuttoning it and putting it on over his t-shirt. "Nancy thinks of everything. She irons, too. I'm going to have to tell Maddie about that."

Don chuckled. "Yeah, no, if you know what's good for you, friend. Sometimes Nancy out-thinks even me. Wives can be like that."

Jim busied himself feeding and watering Lola. "Well, partner, Lola is raring to go. We should get going, too."

Jim put Lola on her leash, and the threesome made for the diner. They caught a break in traffic and sprinted across the busy highway ahead of cars humming by.

The diner's parking lot was almost empty.

Lola's nose swept back and forth along the pathway to the diner. She snuffled and snorted and her tail wagged with the force of a strong wind.

"Oh-oh. I think she recognizes a scent," Jim warned Don.

Don pushed on the door.

The cowbell clattered.

Lola burst past the door, and, nose to floor, yanked on the leash in a try to make for the kitchen.

The cowbell clanged again, and the door swished closed behind them.

Jim commanded the dog to heel.

Reluctantly, Lola gave up the familiar scent, and they made their way to a four-top.

"Sit, Lola. Sit."

Lola sat only long enough to fool Jim before she scurried off, dragging the leash behind her. She ignored Jim's call. Her toenails clicked on the flooring. She slipped and disappeared around the end of the counter.

A disembodied voice called out from the kitchen. "Bring back my shoe!"

Lola pranced out of the kitchen and made for Jim's table in jig time. Her tail wagged so hard it almost shook off.

A woman chased after the nimble dog.

"Mister, if you're going to bring a dog in here, you should train her not to steal the server's shoe." Chewing-gum clicked and snapped.

A chastised Lola dropped the shoe. It

thumped at Jim's feet. She plopped down on his foot and looked up at him. Her tail swept the front of his leg, pleased she found Maddie for him.

"Good girl, Lola. I'm sorry, miss. She's only a puppy. I haven't been able to spend a lot of time with her. The bad habits she picked up come from the black Lab she shares an apartment with. I'm Jim, by the way. This is my friend Don. You already met Lola."

Lola snorted and looked up at Maddie with a pleased expression.

Jim lowered his voice. "Where's Luz? Is she here? Where are your partners in crime?" And finally— "What the hell is going on? You never told me you were working a case."

He looked across at Don to confirm he didn't know anything.

Maddie cast a worried glance around the diner. "We were supposed to meet Luz here. She never showed. We think someone has kidnapped her. We've got eyes on a yellow cargo van. It comes and goes at all hours of the day and night. We checked it out and heard voices in the back. We think someone has shanghaied Luz in a human trafficking operation."

Maddie wiggled her foot into her sneaker.

Lola nuzzled her ankle with a cold nose.

Jim called to the dog. "Lola. Stop that. Sit."

The diner was beginning to fill with anglers eager to get an early start on the day.

"I have to get back to work. The usual, gentlemen?"

Maddie spun around and headed to the

back of the house.

Lola moved to scamper after her.

"Lola. No. Stay."

It took the dog substantial effort to obey. She squirmed and wriggled and wanted to go play with Maddie the instant she recognized her.

After only a few minutes, a server showed up with a plate. "The cook fried some bacon for your dog. I hope you don't mind."

Jim looked across the table at a grinning Don. "I don't feed my dog at the table."

Don rolled his eyes. "Of course not. I should have known."

He addressed the server. "Lola wants you to thank the cook, young lady. Emma, is it?"

Don reached for a warm bit of bacon and moved his hand beneath the table.

Lola didn't need to see the movement twice. She moved to sit beside Don and the treats.

Jim shook his head at the antics of both of them. "Are you trying to steal my dog? If your daughter finds out there's a new girl in your life—"

Their food arrived, and conversation ceased. Both men began eating like it was their last meal.

Maddie stuck her head through the pass-thru and waved to get Jim's attention. She gestured out the window at the unseen yellow step-van pulling into the lot.

"We have company, Don. Get us two to go and meet me on the bench outside. Come, Lola. Time to go."

Chapter 9

Jim **took a seat** outside in the shade at the side of the diner. He pushed his cap back. Behind dark glasses, his eyes moved to check out the van. He snapped a photo of the plate, hoping he could convince Don to run it.

"Come, Lola. Walk time."

The eager pup took up her position at Jim's side, and the pair strolled through the parking lot. He circled around the back of the diner, stopping occasionally to allow Lola to sniff and explore the surroundings.

With the pair out of sight, Don exited the diner and took over lookout duty in front of it. He observed two women approaching the van's driver side. "Now what is this?" One wasn't very old, maybe fifteen or sixteen. He didn't recognize her. The driver rolled down his window. The teenager leaned in and began laughing and giggling. It dawned on him. Emma. The other one had to be Emma. Her last name was on the tip of his tongue—Mayberry. That was it. Emma Mayberry.

He checked out the girl one more time. He twigged suddenly and recognized Anya. Doing more than a passing resemblance to a teenager. From what he could tell, the driver was quite taken. The other woman kept back, as though on guard for Anya. He wondered if either of them was armed. His concern abated somewhat when he remembered they both worked for Jim on a part-time basis. Both were registered Private Detectives in the state. And both were probably armed.

Jim came into view from behind the diner. Lola made a beeline for the women, tugging Jim after her.

Anya dropped to her knees and began petting the dog. "What's his name?"

"Lola. A female. I think she likes you. Come on, Lola. We've had our walk. It's time for some shade."

A reluctant Lola followed Jim to the bench where Don waited.

"That's both of them," Jim said. "Emma and Anya."

Jim mumbled and sat down.

Don pretended to ignore the antics of the women. "I figured the other one was Emma. I almost didn't recognize Anya in that get-up. I think she's playing at being bait. If she is, she's doing one hell of a job."

Jim let it be known he wasn't happy with the situation. If Luz was here—if Luz had been kidnapped—if Maddie and her crew were in danger—if, if, if.

"Dammit Don. Why didn't that woman tell me Luz was coming?"

"There's no sense worrying about it, Nash.

Our job is to run backup, not to interfere. From what I've seen, the women have everything well in hand. Besides, what could we do?"

Jim knew his friend was right. "Well—"

"Well, what? I have a plan," Don admitted.

Jim's attitude changed immediately. "You do?"

Why hadn't he come up with one himself.

Don stood up. "I do. Bring Lola."

He led Jim and the dog around the back of the diner, where he explained the plan. When they came out, Don had Lola. Jim took the long way around the back of the van. He kept out of sight of the driver.

Don waited patiently for the agreed-upon wave.

When it came, Don and Lola strolled toward the back of the van. He bent, linked his hands, and Jim stepped into them. He grunted and hoisted Jim up.

"It's done. Down."

The two men retreated to their campsite. "Car or RV?"

"It has to be the RV. We'll fit in better. Everyone is driving around in one."

They walked across the highway and Jim started the RV. He steered for the exit to the highway, where he parked and waited. "Stakeout," he announced. "We don't have donuts."

Don went into the back and rummaged through a cooler. He handed off a giant-sized cookie. "Tricia makes these."

Jim mumbled past a mouthful of the soft oatmeal treat. "Mmm. Even better than a donut. Home-made. You gonna put the coffee on too?"

"Don't push it, Nash. I just handed you a home-made treat courtesy of my daughter. That ought to hold you for now."

Don brought up the cellphone tracking app on his phone. "Aren't these newfangled phones wonderful things? I don't even need a warrant for your phone since I have your permission."

Jim swallowed a mouthful of cookie. "Don't bug me while I'm taste-testing Tricia's home baking skills. Here we go."

The yellow step-van pulled out of the diner's lot, heading north.

"Where do you think they're going? Magic City?"

Jim took the hint and continued to wait. "I know we don't look suspicious in the camper, but I think we should take our time since we can track them remotely."

Don propped the phone up on the dash as a familiar vehicle pulled out of the lot behind the van. "Isn't that Maddie's car?"

Jim looked up from enjoying his cookie. "It is, but she's not driving. It's Emma. And that looks like Anya in the passenger seat. Dammit, Boyle, what are those women up to?"

Chapter 10

Don Boyle looked across at his friend, Jim, sitting in the driver's seat. He recognized the expression locked on the man's face and knew it wasn't good. "I know what you're thinking, Nash."

Jim's hand was on its way to finding the shift lever.

"Don't do it." Don reached across for the keys hanging out of the ignition. He switched off the RV, emphasizing his command. "Just sit for a bit. Chances are they're following the same prey we're tracking. If they're not, it won't matter. Stay busy eating that cookie. It will make Trish happy when I tell her how much you enjoyed it."

Both pairs of eyes moved to the phone on the dash. The red triangle moved slowly north on the Overseas Highway display.

"You're right. I shouldn't have tried to jump the gun. Emma—"

Don didn't give him time to finish. "From what I witnessed in the diner parking lot, Emma can take care of herself and Anya both. She had an excellent shooting position if

Anya needed that kind of help."

Don reached across for the key and turned it. "Let's go. While we're chasing after these guys, you can tell me all about Emma and Friday setting fire to the van. You know, that van Anya drove cross-country from Mexico? You were in it, remember?"

"Don't bug me, man. I'm busy driving with a Miami detective in the seat beside me, and he has ulterior motives in mind."

Jim took his eyes off the road to look across at Don. "Are you retired yet?" he asked, knowing the answer.

Don returned the look and raised an eyebrow.

That was all Jim needed to needle the man. "In that case, you're gonna have to read us our rights. What do you say, Lola?"

The dog didn't appear to care in the slightest. She was in her bed, napping in the back of the RV.

"They're turning off the highway. Now, where are they going? Is Maddie's car turning too?"

Jim sat up in the seat, trying to see over the line of vehicles in front. "I guess we'll know when we get there, partner."

The red triangle disappeared.

"Shit." Jim reached for the phone and went to smack it. He slapped the dash instead.

"How was the charge on the phone, Nash?"

Jim picked up the phone. The low battery

light flashed and died. The phone was dead. "Apparently not so good. Now what?"

"We know where they turned," Don said. "We'll check it out."

It took longer than Jim was comfortable with getting to the turnoff to chase after the yellow step-van. He braked late, and the van rocked around the corner.

Don made to brace himself. "Take it easy, Nash."

Jim silently cursed his bad luck for not making sure the phone was charged. But then, he was supposed to be fishing, not chasing after two of his neighbors. And Maddie.

"Damn those women, Boyle. What are they up to this time? They're supposed to be on a getaway, not orchestrating a plan to rescue someone."

"This time? You mean this has happened before?" Don laughed. He knew better. "You're put out because they didn't tell you about it. They must have thought it was going to be easy."

Jim wasn't buying it. "Luz saved our bacon in Mexico. Maddie should have told me. She saw the video just like you did. She knew about Luz."

That wasn't strictly true, though. He never sat down with Maddie and explained the whole Mexico deal. He hadn't seen the need. He figured the cash he brought home was enough, and anything more would be wasted.

Well, here he was, in it up to his neck again. In what might well be a human trafficking operation, if Maddie was right. And Luz was one of the victims.

What the hell was Maddie doing working in a diner? Still, he suspected that if it wasn't a part of the deal, she wouldn't be there. If it hadn't been for Don's late-night coffee run and Lola's fetish for Maddie's sneaker—

Jim found himself back at square one. "Where the hell is that damned van? And where did those women get to?"

Don pointed. "There. Slow down. Slow down and stop." He gestured to a small motel coming up fast. He recognized a familiar car in the parking lot. It was Maddie's.

Jim slowed, but he ignored Don's entreaty to stop and kept going.

"Check it out. Is the van there?" He went past the motel and slowed.

"In the back, maybe. Stop. I'll find out."

Jim pulled over to let Don out before proceeding to the dead end. He backed the RV up and turned around in the narrow street. He cursed out loud again at his stupidity for not keeping his phone charged.

The motel was older. Probably 60s vintage. A single story with a sloping roof. More than likely a lot cheaper than those fronting the highway or the water. It would be a good place to do things you wanted to keep out of the way of glaring lights and anyone looking.

Jim looked down the street and spotted Boyle. He was past the motel. Waving frantically. He slowed to pick him up. Lola greeted him like a long-lost friend.

"The van is there," Don said. "In back, like we thought."

He pulled a phone out of his pocket and placed it on the dash.

"Is your charge cable handy?" he asked.

"Nope. Not a chance," Jim admitted.

"Well, we better find one. I replaced your phone with mine. Maybe there's a cable in Maddie's car."

"You going to knock on the door and ask?"

"No, detective," Don said. "I'm going to toss their car. Back in a jiff."

Don returned with a grin, holding out a cord. "Success. They'll never miss it. Now let's regroup and get coffee."

Jim pulled into the huge parking lot across the highway from the turnoff. They wouldn't stand out. There were plenty of other RVs in the lot.

"What are you doing? There's no coffee—"

Jim climbed out of the driver's seat and made for the back of the RV. Lola greeted him with an enthusiastic woof.

"Keeping expenses down. Want some?"

Don sensed Jim was worried about the women in the car. He figured all three of them were likely staying at the same motel as the occupants of the yellow step-van. Perhaps they had met there.

Jim made sure Lola had water before returning to the driver's seat with two quick go-mugs of coffee. "Lola is going need a walk soon."

"If that crap phone of yours would charge,

we'd be good to go."

"It's only been five minutes. Ten at the most. Who's in a hurry now? Besides, the van is parked."

Don gestured across the highway. "Apparently not."

The step-van pulled out onto the highway with Maddie's car in pursuit.

"Shit. And there goes her car. Who's driving? Check the phone. Check the phone."

Chapter 11

Jim rammed the shifter into drive and gunned it toward the exit. He cranked the wheel. The unstable RV swayed from side to side. In the back, Lola barked, making her displeasure known. The highway was blocked with cars in both directions. He hit the brakes, hard. The RV rocked back and forth. With no room to pull into traffic, he was left to pound the steering wheel in frustration.

"Nose it out, Jim. Someone is bound to let you in."

Jim slowly eased the RV into oncoming traffic. No one stopped. No one honked. The cars barely slowed to move around him.

"The phone's up. We've got contact."

Don propped it on the dash.

Jim nodded and a break in traffic presented itself. "Finally." He relaxed, happy they had a position on the yellow step-van and the car chasing after it. "Now if there was a way to find out who was driving Maddie's car—"

A siren blared behind him. He checked the wing mirror and spotted the flashing blues. He slowed and moved to the side to allow the lit-up cruiser to pass. When it didn't, he groaned.

The cruiser pulled in behind him.

"Shit. He wants us. The jig is up. Hands on the dash, Boyle."

Jim grinned across at him and made sure his own hands were in plain sight on the steering wheel.

A female voice floated through the RV's window.

"You can relax, gentlemen. This is a courtesy stop."

Jim recognized the officer's voice immediately. "Well for crying out loud. You can take your hands off the dash, Don. Officer Leanne Wilson is a former work-mate. We shared a desk up north. A long way north."

Jim got out and accompanied Wilson around the back of the RV.

Don adjusted the wing mirror to keep them in sight.

The former partners went into a huddle. Lips moved, but the roar of passing traffic overpowered the chance to listen in.

Jim got back in the RV and filled Don in on what he learned from Officer Wilson.

"Then Maddie was right. There is a human trafficking operation going on. Your cop told us not to stick our noses in or interfere, didn't she?" Don asked.

Jim checked the mirror and eased into a break in traffic. "Not exactly. I sort of let it slip that we heard about the trafficking. Leanne made sure I knew her superiors wouldn't be happy if they discovered we were involved."

"And?" Don waited.

"I insisted we were down on a fishing trip. She only stopped us because she recognized me when she went by while I was trying to get onto the highway. She turned around and followed us."

"So we're home free. Sounds good to me."

"I'm not so sure, Don. She told me there's something going on. Increased patrols. More stops. You think they're onto the same trafficking deal we're looking at?"

"Did you get her card? Why don't you invite her for a quick breakfast at the diner before she starts her patrol in the morning? Maybe she'll let something slip we can use."

"Already done, my friend. We'll be joining her tomorrow first thing. Now where did that van get to?"

The cursor blinked on the phone. The van was making its way south again. They passed on the highway, going in opposite directions.

"Well look at that. Was that Anya in the passenger seat? I hope she knows what she's doing. Those guys won't be so friendly if they find out she's looking for one of their prey."

Maddie's car passed Nash and Boyle in the RV. "That's Emma. She's hot on their tail, too. I swear, Don, when I get those women home, I'm going to—"

"To what, Nash? Spank them? Call me when that happens. Nancy will want to be there, too."

"All right. All right. But we need a plan, Boyle. What do you say to retiring to the campground and regrouping?"

Jim didn't wait for an answer. When Emma fell in behind the yellow step-van, he turned off the highway and made for their campsite.

Don volunteered to take Lola for a walk while Jim backed the RV into their spot and unfurled the awning. Satisfied, he checked for Don and Lola. With the pair out of sight, he crossed the highway to the diner. The cowbell over the door announced his arrival.

He made his way to a stool at the far end of the counter.

Maddie stuck her head out of the pass-thru and called out. "Where's your dog, mister?"

"My friend is walking her. He's taken quite a shine to the dog. In fact, Lola has taken a shine to him, too."

"Is he feeding her?"

"He is. I suppose that's it. I should know better. At the end of the fishing trip, I might not have a dog."

The fishing trip with no end in sight.

He was regretting bringing Lola along, but it wasn't because the two of them were getting along. He was more concerned that the dog would end up getting in the way. He didn't want her getting hurt because he wasn't able to take care of her.

The cowbell clanged again, and Don and Lola traipsed in. Lola glued her nose to the floor. Her tail was at high mast, waving frantically. "I think she smells someone she knows, and I don't mean you. She's looking for that familiar shoe," Don said.

Don and the dog joined them at the

counter, and Jim regarded his friend.

Lola sat between them, looking up hopefully from one to the other. She moved to slink off in the kitchen's direction.

Jim put a foot on her leash.

She tugged at it and returned to sit on the floor.

"You set her after me when you discovered I wasn't in the RV, didn't you?" Jim asked.

"Lola and I aren't a detective team for nothing, Nash. We know our business, don't we, Lola?" Don reached to scratch an ear and Lola appeared to grin up at him.

"Are you trying to steal my dog, Boyle?"

"I don't think I'm going to have to, Nash. Lola just might follow me home."

He swung around on the stool and faced Jim.

"Now, what are we going to do?"

Chapter 12

J im considered his options. There weren't
many. He couldn't ignore what he had seen.
He couldn't ignore what was going on. If Luz
was involved, he had to act. He couldn't allow
the girl—she had to be a woman by now—to
be trapped in a human trafficking operation.
And with Don asking—

"I didn't know Maddie and her friends
were down here to help Luz, I swear," Jim said.
"Now that I know, I have to get Luz out of
whatever it is she got herself railroaded into."

He held up a hand, not permitting Don to
interrupt.

"You can head home. I'd appreciate it if
you'd take Lola with you. She's not like Friday.
I can't depend on her. I'll keep the RV. I'll pick
up a burn phone to attach to the step-van. So
far, it looks like it's the only vehicle involved."

He went on.

"You know I can rely on Maddie. Emma,
too. Anya is the unknown. I'd load her into the
trunk of your car, but she'd never allow it. If
you knew how stubborn that one was—"

It was Don's turn to hold up a hand to halt

Jim. "Partner, we're in this together whether or not you like it. Right, Lola?"

Lola woofed. She liked the sound of this human's voice.

"Besides, we both know if Nancy found out I deserted you, she'd have my hide, wouldn't she, Lola?"

The dog nudged Don's thigh and looked up at Jim, as if to ask why she didn't belong to this new male.

"She'd probably have both our hides. Now, this is the way I see it, Boyle."

Jim recapped where they were, even though they had little to go on.

"We've got Maddie's word that Luz is down here. Or she soon will be. In the meantime, they've been turned on to a human trafficking operation. Whether Luz is involved, no one knows. We've got the yellow step-van and we know where they're staying."

Jim hesitated before going on, but not because he needed to catch his breath. He had no idea what would come next.

"About that motel. We need to get a room. Or at the very least, we should stake it out. The traffickers might be staying there, but we don't know what else is going on. What do you think, Boyle?"

It didn't matter what Boyle thought. He'd do it even if Boyle didn't approve.

"This is turning into one of our more expensive fishing trips, Nash. Okay. Let's get the lead out. We'll switch out the RV for my car, but I'm warning you. If Nancy's favorite mode of transport gets shot up, it's on you and Lola."

Lola woofed, loud this time, as though in agreement with Don. Her tail wagged up a storm.

Don said, "Then that seals it, right, Lola? We'll go check in to that shady motel and settle in for ice-cold drinks in the back forty. We'll be able to keep watch over the trash blowing in."

The crew headed back to the RV.

Jim rounded up Lola's bed and bowls and some food. He added a couple of toys and tossed it all into the trunk of Don's car. By the time he was ready, Don was back with Lola. Both were huffing and puffing.

"You ran her?"

"More like she ran me, Nash. I need to get in better shape."

"You kids can take a nap when we get to our new accommodations. I checked in with the camp office to let them know we'd be away for a couple of nights, in case they thought we checked out."

They slammed doors, and Don made for the highway. "By any chance did you notice the name of that place?"

The tab for the Largo Key Motel was 80 bucks in advance for two room keys, a cot, and a pail for an ice bucket.

Jim bumped and rolled the cot over broken cement and halted at the door. "Nice place you got here, Boyle."

"No prob, Nash, considering it's all the fault of your crew. If I bring bedbugs home, you'll all be in Nancy's bad graces."

"Nah. I'll leave Friday for a few extra days—oh, I better not. No sense in Maddie's dog laying down with fleas."

The men chuckled as they entered the room.

Jim pulled the cot in behind him.

The layout wasn't great, but it smelled of fresh paint. Outdoor carpet covered the floor and cheap-looking new furniture squatted on the carpet. Even the single cot would be a tight fit.

"It's not so bad."

Jim pulled open the door to the back of the motel. It overlooked an expanse of green shaded by palms and miscellaneous greenery. Bright bougainvillea hung from divider fencing between the rooms.

"We've got our own patio. What do you say I take Lola for a walk and check the place out? You can fill that bucket with motel ice and our beer."

"I'd say you've got a crush on my dog. Does Nancy know? Or better yet, does Trish suspect?"

"I'll never tell. Now where did I put Lola's leash?"

Jim dug out the bowls and filled one with water. He observed Don and Lola on their walk. Don gave her enough leash to allow her to sniff and snort her way around the back of the motel. He commanded her to heel before they made their way around the front and out of sight.

He collected the tin pail and picked up ice for Lola. He left the extra in the pail for the beer and carted two lawn chairs into the shade of twin palms in the motel's back yard. He whistled when he saw Don and Lola returning.

Don dropped the leash and Lola ran to sit at Jim's feet.

"So you still miss me, do you?" He reached to scratch an ear. "I was thinking you deserted me for Boyle over there."

Don set Lola's water bowl beneath the palms. "This is a pretty good setup, Nash. We have a line of sight into all the rooms from here."

Don cracked two beers, and the men chugged the cold, refreshing amber liquid in the evening's fading light. "How long do you think it will be?"

"I expect them any time. Probably with our girls not far behind."

Chapter 13

Jim gestured with his chin toward the end of the motel.

Don nodded.

The yellow step-van made its way around the end of the Largo Key Motel and into the back parking area. It halted and reversed. The piercing sound of the back-up alarm sounded to announce the end of the journey. The rear tires bumped the cement barrier, and the van rocked back and forth. The backup horn halted and driver and passenger exited and slammed the doors.

The men kept up their conversation through the screeching.

"You'd think they'd disable that. Want another beer?"

"Not right now. I think I'll take Lola for a bit of a walk. She needs the exercise and I need a better look."

"Well, if you need me, I'll be here with the cooler."

Don reached in, rattled the ice, and replaced the empty beer in his hand with a fresh one. He waved it in Jim's direction. "Just in case."

Jim allowed Lola to take the lead.

She covered the ground in the motel's back forty as fast as he permitted. She sniffed and snorted and wagged her tail and pulled Jim in the direction of the yellow van. He allowed her to smell the tires and then commanded her to heel. He walked her between the van and the room. Lola halted at the room's open door. She snorted and looked up at Jim. He tugged her away and together they took the long way back to the palm trees and a waiting Don.

"Well? What did Lola suss out?" Don asked.

"The two men. Lots of clothes scattered around the room. Bags and suitcases and general mayhem throughout."

"Like they're searching for valuables."

"Probably. Which means—"

"People. People missing their luggage. Maybe never seeing it again. Did Lola pick up any sounds in the van? Noise? Any noise?"

"She didn't twig to anything that I could tell. She halted at the open door to the room and I took a listen. I noticed the mess in the room right off. I didn't want to look suspicious, so I pulled her away."

"Any chance we can replace the phone on the roof?"

"Not right away. Maybe later after dark if they're still here. Judging by the condition of the room, I'm thinking they've been busy boys. We should probably take a better look the next time they leave."

They were moving people. It was obvious

now. But were they moving illegals, or migrant farm workers? Was Luz involved somehow? Surely Anya hadn't convinced Maddie to come down on a whim.

"We need to get into that room," Jim said.

Chapter 14

Don's eyes roamed over the motel. It wasn't a place he would choose to check into if he didn't have to. "Cripes, Nash. What do you pay Maddie that she has to front for a room in a dump like this?"

Jim threw side-eye Don's way, interrupting his recon of the street and the approach to the motel. "I don't pay her—"

"I can tell. I need to have a talk with that woman."

"Look, Boyle. You know we're equal partners in the business. She can walk into the bank any day of the week and leave me hanging any which-way she chooses."

Don nodded and left it alone.

"We need to scout this thing. How are we going to work it?"

They slogged their way up the street, pretending to be a couple of tourists. Lola tugged at her leash, nose to ground, tail straight up. Jim called her to heel, and she obeyed instantly. "Good girl, Lola."

Nash reached to scratch at the dog's ear. She rewarded him with a cool wet nose against his hand.

"Does Maddie know she has competition?" Boyle asked.

"She does, just like you know Friday is your competition for Tricia. Are we even now?"

The men grinned and returned to scouting the motel.

"I'm going to work my way around the back to check on the yellow step van," Don said. "Are you good in front?"

Jim nodded, and Don headed down the uneven sandy alley to find the back of the motel. Jim halted just past an old, squat palm tree replete with its untrimmed skirt of dead fronds.

"Now would be a good time for a piddle, Lola. What do you think?"

The dog obliged, and he used the opportunity to check out the front parking lot. It was bare of cars but for Maddie's.

"I wonder if she's home."

He looked down at Lola and decided she wasn't. Based on experience, the dog would champ at the bit to get to her and her sneakers. He smiled, recalling the first time he introduced Lola and Maddie. The puppy scurried back to Jim and dropped Maddie's sneaker at his feet before returning to Maddie in the doorway, wanting to play with someone new.

Enough reminiscing.

It was time to get to work. He tied off Lola's leash before taking a last look at the lot. He used Maddie's car as cover as he made his way toward it.

A gunshot rang out. Sand and gravel exploded at his feet. He drew his weapon and ran for the car. He collapsed behind the front, intending to use the engine block for cover. Another shot sounded. It pinged through the tin and whizzed by.

Well, it looks like we're into it now.

Boyle rushed around the side of the motel and joined him behind Maddie's car. "Where's it coming from?"

Jim gestured with the muzzle of his handgun. "Looks like the end unit. Where the van was parked when we checked the place out yesterday."

Another single shot banged into the car.

"Maddie is going to be some pissed when she finds out what you did to her car, Nash."

"Technically, it's not me doing the doing. You think they have long guns?"

Boyle shrugged his shoulders. "If they did, you'd think they'd have brought them out by now."

A bad-luck burst of automatic gunfire interrupted Don's thinking. "I guess we know now."

Jim dialed in full auto on his modified Model 17 and answered by emptying the 9-shot magazine in the room's direction. He released the magazine and reached for one of the 30-shot magazines he carried. It clicked into place. Satisfied, he peeked around the front of Maddie's car.

Don's phone chose that moment to ring. A photo of Nancy showed up on the screen. "Shit.

It's the wife. I have to take this, Nash."

A burst of gunfire exploded and then went silent.

Don chose the lull to take the call. He got out, hello, dear, an instant before Jim pulled the trigger. A rat-a-tat-tat directed at the room halted. He was half-way through the magazine.

"Is everything all right, Don?" Nancy wondered.

"Oh yes. I'm a little busy, dear. Do you need anything?"

Jim emptied the rest of his magazine and loaded the second.

"No. I just called to see how the fishing was going."

Jim let go with another burst of full-automatic fire.

"Is that Jim helping out?" Nancy wanted to know.

"Actually, it's the other way around. I'm helping him out."

"That's good to know. Let me know if you need me."

Don pocketed the phone.

The parking lot was silent.

The sun beat down.

Waves of heat reflected off the asphalt.

"What do you think?"

"I think our fishing cover is blown with Nancy," Jim said. "But yeah, we're done. Let's go see."

They made their way to the front of the motel and walked single-file to the end room. Jim kicked the bullet-riddled door open. It fell back on its hinges with a satisfying thud.

Don placed a hand on his shoulder and they entered the room together.

Two bodies confronted them. A set of keys lay on the floor between the bodies.

"Let's go see what these get us."

Together, they made their way around the end room to the back side of the motel. They kicked open doors to reveal empty rooms. They confronted the last door. Kicked at it. Screams greeted them. They kicked together, and the door flew open.

Half a dozen women confronted them, swinging chairs and lamps and a shower rack.

The men backed out of the room and regrouped.

"You speak Spanish?"

"Poquito, cabrón."

Jim addressed the women. Told them he was a private cop. Explained that he was there looking for his partner. Asked about Luz.

Rapid-fire Spanish from the women assaulted his ears. He held up his hands. "Lenta. Lenta. Slow, por favor."

Sirens sounded, getting closer.

"Nash. We have to get out of here. Now."

"Señoritas. Las migras. We have to go."

Don opened the back of the van and Jim got in. He gestured for the women to follow. When the last one climbed aboard, he closed one door and left the other unlatched and open.

"Silencio, por favor. Quiet." He put a finger to his lips for emphasis.

Don made his way to the driver's seat and

steered the van out of the motel's abandoned parking lot and onto the street. He halted beside the palm tree, exited, and untied Lola. She bounded into the back of the van with Jim and slid to a halt on the aluminum floor.

Female oohs and aahs greeted her.

Lola's tail wagged at unfamiliar hands rubbing her ears and tickling her stomach. She was about to roll onto her back when Jim called.

"Lola. Heel."

Reluctantly, the dog obeyed, but her tail didn't. It continued to wag, sweeping the van's floor in a wide swath.

Don eased the van down narrow, sandy back lanes toward the highway. Jim slid the divider open. "How are we going to find Maddie and Luz, Boyle? Any ideas?"

A babble of Mexican voices confronted Jim.

One woman tugged at his shirt. In halting English, she described what sounded like a location.

Chapter 15

It **was almost dark** when Nancy remembered she promised Melanie she would return to the Retro Owl to complete her purchases of the day before. She wasn't looking forward to returning to the scene of the crime and the robbery Friday helped to foil.

It wasn't the idea of the robbery so much as it was the firearm that was involved. Even so, she collected Tricia and Friday from the back yard and waited while her daughter changed into one of the retro outfits she picked out yesterday.

Friday, already decked out in his scarf, preened by the front door.

"Yes, Friday. I know, I know. It's car ride time."

The big black Lab woofed, anxious to get going and eager to feel the wind in his face.

Tricia finally arrived and Friday woofed again. The front door opened, and he bounded for the car. He scrambled past the door Nancy held open for him and jumped into the back seat. He took up his favorite position.

"He never tires of that back seat, does he? I

think he claims it for his own just so he can hit me with that cold, wet nose."

Nancy got in behind the wheel and Friday did just that.

Trish giggled and reached to give him a pat and all three settled into their seats. They retraced their steps to downtown Magic City and the Retro Owl.

"Do you think Melanie will be there today, mom?"

Friday's ears perked up immediately. He remembered the chicken tenders the other female fed him as a treat. He nosed Nancy's neck again, hoping to hurry the drive to the treats.

"I hope so. It will make settling up a lot easier. I brought the tags, but even so— here we are."

She pulled into the same spot, and the threesome got out. Melanie saw them and rushed out to greet everyone.

Friday made a fuss and Melanie blushed and led them into the store.

"That spoiled dog is looking for treats again. If he doesn't get them, he'll pout."

"No problem. I hoped you'd come back when I was here. I picked up a little something special just for my savior." She held up a bag of dog treats. "Do you think these are all right?"

Nancy nodded. "They certainly are."

Friday walked circles around Melanie, sniffing and snorting.

"He's such a spoiled brat, aren't you, Friday?"

The dog didn't care. He was busy kissing up to Melanie and the treats, not necessarily in that order. Melanie's eyes moved from the dog back to Nancy. "Mrs. Boyle, can I ask a personal question?"

"Of course. After yesterday, you can ask me anything."

"What's that strange outline in your bra?"

You mean this old thing?" Nancy reached into her blouse with her left hand and pulled out a magazine. "It's my backup."

The women laughed.

Friday scurried off to sit by the counter, where he kept a watchful eye on the door. He waited, patient yet eager for the female to show up with the treats.

"I promised yesterday I'd come back to settle the bill after the fuss was over. I brought the tags." She reached into her bag and slid them across the counter.

"That was quite a shock yesterday, Mrs. Boyle. I'm not sure I'm over it yet." Melanie's eyes wandered toward the store's open door.

Friday nudged her thigh, and she forgot about the door and reached into the bag of treats.

"How did it go after the police arrived?" Nancy asked.

"I did exactly what you told me to do. I dropped the shoe and put up my hands. They took it from there. They wanted to know who helped me subdue the guy, but I convinced them I did it by myself. I don't think they believed me, but there were no witnesses, so—"

"You did good. I'm glad you kept my daughter out of it." Nancy didn't explain that her husband was a police lieutenant. She didn't think it necessary.

"Did you see the pictures from yesterday?" Melanie asked.

"What's this? Pictures? Of what?"

"Mostly of you and your daughter and faithful Friday."

"Oh. Social media. I don't pay attention to that."

"Well, you should see what's on insta," Melanie said.

Tricia's ears perked up at the mention of the site. "Mom, that's cool. What do they say, Melanie?"

The clerk reached for her phone and called up her account. "Take a look." She turned her phone over to Nancy. Intrigued, she scrolled through the posts.

"You even have your own hash tag, Mrs. Boyle. Look."

Nancy scrolled through tagged images of Jim's convertible. She and Tricia were wearing the clothes they had put on in the store. The images made the two of them resemble 50s movie stars while their spoiled and pampered pet lounged in the back of the car.

"Oh-oh. Jim will never let us live this down, dear. His car has taken center stage. At least there's no mention of the robbery."

Melanie nodded. "That's probably because you beat a hasty retreat before people knew what went down. You look pretty cool, though. And that car."

"You're too kind. I think you just made my daughter's day, though. Right Friday?"

The dog didn't care in the slightest. He nosed Melanie, and she freed up another treat while she slid the bill across the counter.

Nancy paid and prepared to leave.

"All right. Well, we should be off. Maybe we'll take a turn down the main drag and do a loop. What do you think, Tricia?"

Tricia whooped and made for the car.

Friday, ever the conscientious guard dog, took off after the girl.

Nancy thanked Melanie, and they were off.

Chapter 16

Jim and Don relaxed in the evening shade provided by the twin palms.

The van remained where it was parked. Loud voices emanated from the room from time to time and quieted.

"Either they're arguing over something, or their plan is falling apart— oops, there they go."

The doors on the van slammed and it made for the front of the motel.

"I'll go check it out. Wait until I get back."

Don headed around to the front of the motel.

Jim made for their room. He left Lola snoozing beneath the trees.

"All clear. Where's Lola?"

Jim gestured toward the palms. "Our detective trainee is having a snooze. Kind of like Friday and I do in the office from time to time."

"Ha. According to Maddie, the two of you sleep in there more than you're awake."

"I'll spank that girl for revealing our secrets."

"Sure, you will. Give the Boyle family a call

when you do. We want to bear witness to your screams of submission.”

Jim fiddled with the lock on the room's door and turned the handle. “We're in.

Clothes and suitcases and bags and cardboard boxes lay everywhere. All of it appeared well used.

Jim rummaged through dresser drawers. “Nothing. No jewelry. No phones. Nada.”

Don tossed the bed, found nothing, and rearranged the covers.

“They can't be coyotes. The closest border is with Cuba, and that's 90 miles over water.”

Lola stood up and barked. Both men hesitated.

“We better get out of here. I think our friends might be back with fast food.”

Jim locked the door and pulled it shut. He called to the dog. “Come Lola.”

She made a beeline for the two men and halted between them, sniffing hands and nosing legs. The step-van pulled into the parking spot in front of the room. Two men got out with bags of food. Lola moved to explore and sniff the men.

“Sorry about my dog. She's still a puppy and a bit of a handful. Come Lola.”

He patted his thigh and the threesome returned to lawn chairs and palm trees.

One man opened the step-van's rear door and climbed in. His partner exited their room with a broom and began pushing everything out onto the ground. When they finished, they hauled it all into the room.

"We were right. They'll be going through it for valuables."

"How many do you think they got away with?"

"No idea, but they're experienced by the look of it. I wonder how long they've been running the scam?"

The men retreated into the room and the door crashed shut.

"They're going to be busy for a while. Should we change out the phone on the roof?"

Jim and Don made for their own room as Lola trailed after them. She stopped and sniffed and was well on her way to more exploring by the time Jim noticed.

"Lola. Come."

The dog ignored him and continued on her way around the back of the motel.

"Lola. Come."

Jim got no response from the dog.

Don called and didn't get one, either.

"She's fired, Nash. If we can't depend on a dog, who can we depend on?"

Don answered his ringing cell phone. It was Nancy, wanting to know how the fishing was going and if they'd be bringing anything home.

"You have little faith in your menfolk, dear. How would you like a dog?"

Don explained how Jim was having a hard time with Lola and how worried he was about her. "She's not like Friday in the slightest. He can't depend on her, and he's concerned she'll get hurt."

"So then, he asked you if you want a dog?"

Nancy inquired.

Don hesitated before replying. "Well, not exactly. All I can tell you is that he's having second thoughts. And don't mention anything to Trish. I don't want her to get her hopes up. How are you enjoying the car?"

"We're out for a drive as we speak. Friday is enjoying the wind in his face. Tricia is all dolled up like a 50s child star. We might even be on the internet. Insta-something-or-other."

"I'll check it out later. It's time to reel in some fish. Oh, and be sure to let Tricia know Jim loves her baking." Don hung up in time to greet Lola and Jim.

"You lied to your wife. Shame on you."

"You would too if she found out I was working on what you promised was a fishing trip."

"I have news for you, Don. If Nancy isn't deaf, she heard the gunfire. I suspect she's on to both of us by now. And anyway, we can buy fresh fish on the way home. What are we going to do about these two?"

"It's not too late. Let's go to the diner for a coffee. Lola hasn't stolen any shoes recently."

"Very funny."

They pulled out of the motel lot trailed by the step van. It followed them to the diner.

"Great minds think alike."

"Yeah. And the usual suspects are hot on their trail, too."

The three vehicles pulled into the diner lot. The van occupants stayed in the van. Emma and Anya hesitated before getting out. It gave

Jim and Don and Lola the opportunity to enter the diner.

The cowbell over the door clanged to welcome them and they made for a four-top at the back. Don took a seat facing the door. Jim sat across from him to monitor the parking lot. The server poured two cups of coffee and went off to wait other tables.

"Our step-van is taking off. Do we follow it, Nash?"

"No. Let's see what the women are up to."

Chapter 17

J im and Don took over a four-top. The two women joined them. Don faced Anya. Jim sat with his back to the door, facing Emma and Don. He kept busy checking the parking lot and the highway, looking for the van in case it returned.

A reflection on the diner wall shifted Boyle's attention from the people at the tables. His eyes moved to the door.

A disembodied hand followed by an arm reached through the partially open door.

The hand went up. Found the cow bell. Gripped it to prevent it from sounding an alarm.

A woman followed the arm past the door into the diner.

Already her eyes were scanning the crowd in the diner. The door closed silently behind her. The hand released the bell.

Immediately Don recognized what the woman was doing. She was assessing. Casing the joint.

She dismissed the server first. Her eyes turned to him and glanced away too quickly.

They returned and hovered for an instant too long before moving away a second time. She glanced back and caught him studying her.

He'd been made. How did she know?

The woman's eyes left him to move over the rest of the crowd. This time, she ignored him completely. Of course. She already made him as a cop. Or something. He reached to pat his sidearm, providing a measure of comfort. He didn't know what was going down, but he was ready.

"Nash. Check the door. The woman just made me," he said.

"What? Who? I didn't hear the bell."

"There was no bell."

"No bell? It should have woke the dead."

Jim turned. Gave the woman the once-over.

A well-worn backpack hung off a shoulder. Faded khaki pants. A jacket with pockets. A bandana holding brown hair in check prevented it from cascading over her shoulders.

"You're right. She's a looker." He turned for a better look. This time, he recognized the woman. His chair scraped the floor. "It's her. Don. It's Luz."

Jim stood up. His chair tipped. Don made a grab for Lola's leash. The woman's eyes flashed recognition and then she was blocked from sight as Jim rushed to her side.

"Santiago." Tears overflowed as Luz recognized him.

He called to Don. "Case closed. Check if Maddie is in the kitchen and get her out of here. Now."

"No sweat. I've got Lola. Take care of Luz and the others. Go."

Wailing sirens sounded in the distance and grew closer.

"Jim. They're early. It's time."

Jim reached to grab Luz. Connected with her backpack. "We need to get out of here before the fireworks start. Come on, Luz. Let's get a move on."

He shoved Anya and Emma in front of him.

Boyle and the dog rushed to make for the kitchen. "I'll bring up the rear with Lola, Nash. Come on, dog. Let's find Maddie."

Unfazed by the excitement, Lola reached the end of her leash. She recognized Maddie's scent and tugged Don toward the kitchen.

"Maddie. It's time to go," Don called.

Startled diner patrons looked up to witness the dash to the diner's side door. Jim shoved it open. It slapped against the side of the building. Lola woofed and pranced out of the kitchen, followed by Maddie. Proud of her accomplishment, the dog chased after all of them. Outside, she sniffed and snorted at the new female in their midst, looking for reassurance she was still top dog.

The women hesitated and slowed. "Don't stop. Keep going. Over the berm. All the way."

Reluctantly, they kept on. Anya chattered to Luz. Don silenced her. "Anya. Shut up. We need to get out of here."

Luz grabbed Anya's wrist and pulled her toward the highway. Sirens screamed and then halted as the contingent of troopers turned off the highway. Squad cars rolled into the diner's parking lot.

"Just in time, folks. Our campsite is across the road. Let's go before traffic gets bad again," Jim said.

"Did anyone notice if the step van was there?"

"It pulled in as we were leaving. I caught a glimpse over my shoulder when I was running out of the kitchen. I think my rep as a cook is done, though."

Maddie eyed the woman. Luz was barely recognizable from what she remembered of the shootout she had witnessed on television. "Luz? I'm so glad to finally meet you. Thank you for helping to get Jim home."

She hugged Luz, and Jim wrapped his arms around both of them. Lola kept circling and sniffing, satisfied she had most likely found a new friend.

Don didn't waste the opportunity.

"We're missing our vehicles. We probably won't get them back until tomorrow. Until then, welcome to Boyle's Hideaway." He slid the camper door open and supervised as everyone made their way into the cramped quarters. He and Lola brought up the rear.

"Have we got everyone, Nash? We better do a body count in case Emma ran out the back door on her way to—"

"She's here, Boyle. Stop picking on one of my girls if you know what's good for you. Right, Lola?"

The dog woofed as nervous laughter echoed through the camper.

"Good girl, Lola."

The dog sat at Don's feet.

Maddie looked at Jim. "What's going on with your dog?"

"I think she wants to be a part of the Boyle family."

"Speaking of the Boyle family, Nash and friends, I seem to remember Emma and Friday were last seen walking, no, scratch that, running from a van that was on fire. An armored van, if I remember correctly. Does anyone know anything about that?"

Jim had warned Emma about Don's ongoing questions about the van and who was involved. She dodged the question and went down on a knee to pet Lola while she changed the subject. "Nah. Couldn't have been me. I've never driven an armored car in my life."

Boyle sighed and Jim shrugged.

Emma smiled. She knew when to shut up.

"All right, you runaways. Your menfolk had to cancel their fishing trip. Is there some reason you didn't tell James here what you were up to? After the gunfire, my wife thinks we were down here robbing a bank in a shootout."

Maddie broke away from the clutch. "That's my fault. We didn't want to warn Jim. I never knew you two would be here on a fishing trip. If I had, I would have told you both."

"I had to set Nancy straight on the phone during a break in the gunfire while Jim was reloading. Unfortunately, he got reloaded before I hung up. It blew our cover. Speaking of which, I need to call home. Not a one of you is to start making plans until I get back."

Chapter 18

Don knocked on the camper door and gestured to Jim. "Nancy wants to talk to you." He put the phone on speaker before handing it over. When Jim hung up, they had a plan.

"All right, people. Here's the deal."

He looked at Luz. Their eyes locked and she nodded. "Nancy Boyle will meet us with a car. All of you will go back with her while Don and I clean up things with some people we met while we were here. We'll try to get Maddie's car and if we can't, it might get hit by lightning. Don, you didn't hear that."

A knock on the camper door disturbed the meeting. Don opened it to find the campground's owner.

"Mr. Boyle. You can't be bringing these women in here unless they sign the guest register. Is that clear?"

Don held up his hands.

"No problem. I don't want to ruffle anyone's feathers. We ran into some old friends. Their car broke down. We've arranged for alternate transportation. My wife should arrive shortly—if that's all right with you."

Satisfied, the man nodded and departed.

"First problem solved, Boyle. Now who's going to go with Nancy?"

The two men made for the picnic table to formulate a plan.

Laughing and giggling in the camper brought them back. "Look at those four. You'd never know Luz was a stranger to most of them only a few hours ago."

A car idled up to the camper. A nervous Jim pulled aside a curtain and recognized its occupants. Nancy exited the car followed by an excited Tricia and Friday.

"The gang's all here now, Boyle. I think we're going to be in trouble for not having any fish."

Tricia and Friday crowded into the camper. It was old home week for the dogs, and it kept everyone amused while Jim and Don met with Nancy at the picnic table.

"Luz and Anya are going to come with me back to the city," she announced. "I made plans for Luz to talk to an immigration lawyer. If she has all the right papers, he says it shouldn't be a problem.

She called to Luz and Jim made introductions when she joined them at the table. Luz reached into her backpack and withdrew an envelope. "I think I have everything."

She made to hand the papers over to Nancy.

"That's all right. We have a meeting to get you to, Luz. I'll explain on the way. Anya will come with us on the drive home. You'll both be staying at our place tonight."

Luz looked at Jim and he nodded.

Satisfied, she sighed. Her whole body collapsed. Jim caught her and settled her gently onto the bench. "You're home now, Luz. Good people care about you. The best. You'll see."

Nancy called to the dogs. "Friday. Lola. Are you coming?"

Tricia trailed after the dogs. Three women and two dogs climbed into Jim's Packard and Nancy hit the button to put the top up. "We're going in style, ladies. All aboard that's getting aboard."

Friday's cold nose nudged the back of Nancy's neck. Lola did the same to Anya in the front seat. Giggles and laughter came from within the Packard as Nancy eased into traffic and headed north.

"Well, that's done, boys and girls. Does anyone want to go fishing?"

When the group returned, they had half a dozen fish to their credit. No one witnessed the pair at the grocery store.

"We should bring the women more often, Boyle. They bring good luck at the grocery store. We actually caught something."

Don grinned furiously.

"I'll put them in the fridge. You're all

invited to a Boyle fish fry tomorrow. Nancy was thinking we were up to no good, and here we are with the prized fish. She'll never believe we didn't raid a grocery store on the way home. Right, people?"

There was no disagreement.

L uz was impressed by Nancy Boyle's fluent Spanish. The two women conversed non-stop all the way home, with few interruptions.

Emma and Anya ended up fast asleep with Tricia and had to be roused.

Even Friday and Lola were bored by the lack of attention.

Luz was able to convince Nancy of the seriousness of her intent to become naturalized. As far as she was concerned, she had all the proper documentation. All she needed was an advocate, and she felt she had one in Nancy Boyle.

Luz had the results she needed to carry out her plan. Thanks to Jim—her personal Santiago—and the money he gifted on the beach in Todos Santos. She turned it into a small fortune. How she'd done it might not have been completely legitimate, but now, with her arrival in America, she was ready to activate her plan. She would dedicate all of her money to it.

For now, she was convinced she could tell no one, even her beloved savior, Santiago. And especially not Anya. The girl was a chatterbox, and untrustworthy because of it. As for Emma, she was an unknown. Maddie might be some help, but she would have to commit time to getting to know her better. She would have to do that for all of them.

Time. She had plenty of that.

Chapter 19

Luz settled in with the Boyle's. Nancy insisted on it. She allowed her to take over the room in the basement. It was more like a castle, even though it resembled none she had ever shared with a Mexican drug lord. It was all hers, Nancy told her, to do with as she saw fit.

The nightmares continued. Luz could control them to some extent with meditation. Having Tricia and Lola helped, too. She considered them both to be her "comfort people". Lola could sense when she was having issues, and never deserted her. Tricia would get lonely for her dog and come looking. Once she found her, she stayed and nattered on. Luz didn't mind. She enjoyed both of them. Actually, she enjoyed the entire family.

She knew Don made her when she entered the restaurant. She made him right off, too. It was her experience. His, too, no doubt. She observed him checking his firearm beneath his shirt. She didn't blame him. He did not know who she was until Jim—Santiago—identified her.

All that didn't matter now. She was one of

the family. She liked that. It made her feel good to be recognized for herself. She didn't miss a single thing about her former country.

Still, she needed to get a job to get back on track. That would be next on her agenda. In the meantime, she would continue to enjoy her new life.

Sometimes on weekends she would ask Nancy to take her to a Mexican mercado where the two would pick out food for a feast. It usually involved inviting the Nash clan. That meant not only Jim and Maddie and Friday, but Anya and Emma, too. She would cook for most of the day, assisted by Nancy, who wanted to learn her recipes, and by Tricia. Come mid to late afternoon, the feast was ready. So were the guests. It pleased her a great deal that she could remember her mother's endless recipes and that she could prepare them just as she had.

It was following one of these feasts that she decided to walk to the store for some ice cream for Lola. Tricia thought it was a grand idea and let her know she'd be coming along.

Don was stuffed and complaining about the weight he was gaining. Nancy had to remind him he needed to push himself away from the table sooner.

Luz laughed and sent Lola off for her leash.

Tricia changed into a summer dress, in an attempt to match the dress Luz was wearing. She rushed downstairs.

"All right. I'm ready," Tricia announced. "Come on, Lola. Ice cream."

Lola knew the sound of those two words

from memory now. She heard them many times. She whined at the front door until it was opened and she tumbled out, stretching her leash and tugging at Tricia's firm grip. The girl called to the dog. "Lola. Heel."

Grudgingly, Lola obeyed.

"That's a pretty dress, Tricia," Luz said.

"Thank you. My mom made it for me. Yours is prettier."

"My mother made mine as well. She sewed for all of us in our family."

Luz didn't dwell on her explanation. Besides, she knew Tricia wouldn't ask. It was just as well she didn't know, anyway.

Lola wasn't interested in wasting time listening to talk about something she didn't understand. She was committed to having ice cream. She had been to the store in search of ice cream so many times she knew the way all by herself.

"Tricia, if we let her off the leash, your dog would wait for us at the store until someone pulled open the door for her," Luz said.

Tricia giggled. "I know. But we can't. I don't trust Lola by herself."

Luz and Tricia traipsed after Lola as she hurried on the familiar route toward the store. She barely stopped to sniff and snort.

"She's so funny. On the way home she'll take her sweet time. We won't be able to drag her back. She is so spoiled, Luz."

The threesome approached the store. An enthusiastic Lola had to be called to heel, and she obeyed. Luz pulled the door open and froze. Tricia bumped into her.

Luz turned to the girl and whispered. "Go home. Take Lola. Do not stop for anyone or anything. Go now."

"But—" the girl began.

"Do what I tell you. Go home now."

Tricia recognized Luz's tone and obeyed without objecting.

A disappointed Lola had to be tugged away from the door, but she obeyed her keeper and heeled. The pair ran away from the store as fast as they could.

Luz entered and made her way to the till. She called to the clerk. "I come for ice cream for dogs. Do you have any?" She kept approaching.

The man with the gun swung it in her direction. His hand wavered and shook.

Not a killer.

Perhaps a drug addict.

She kept walking. The method had served her well in her former country. She was feet away from him.

The nervous clerk eyed her from behind the counter. He was sizing her up. He had dismissed her immediately as ineffectual. A mere woman.

Luz sensed more danger from a mistaken trigger pull than a deliberate attempt to harm anyone. She looked straight at the clerk. She continued to move closer to the armed man.

"Give him what he wants," she said.

The clerk's voice quavered. "He hasn't asked for anything."

Luz turned to the robber. "What do you

want? Tell him."

The gun wavered and returned to point at her. "Money. I need money."

During the exchange the robber allowed Luz to move even closer. She was within striking distance.

"Very well. Tell him, not me."

The robber turned. It was a mistake.

Luz flicked out with her left hand. Smacked the gunman's hand. Knocked it up to point at the ceiling.

She moved in, close.

She liked to be close.

Her left arm came down on his shoulder. It knocked him off balance.

He screamed in pain.

The gun clattered to the floor.

She swept at the feet of the robber and he went down.

She grabbed for the handgun and covered him off. It was light. Maybe even empty.

The clerk came around from behind the counter, baseball bat in hand.

Tires squealed in the parking lot behind the door. The robber's partner.

Luz gripped the handgun with both hands.

She took up a shooting position and covered off the door with her two-handed grip.

She leaned into it.

Nancy Boyle rushed through the door.

Luz observed the handgun down at Nancy's side and the bulge in her blouse. She recognized it for what it was immediately.

Backup.

She dropped the hand holding the robber's gun.

"Tricia told me there was trouble. Are you all right?"

"I'm fine. So is he." Luz gestured to the clerk.

"That's the store owner. Ike, are you all right?"

"I'm fine. You should have seen this one in action."

"Luz. Give me the gun. Go to the car. Now."

The woman did as she was told.

"Wipe the handgun, Ike. Please."

She watched him do it before he cold-cocked the robber with his bat.

"That'll hold him until the police get here."

"No police, Ike. Luz can't be involved."

She knew Ike had a state-of-the-art video system he had just installed. He told her all about it on one of her visits with Lola.

"Can I get a copy of the action before you erase it?" she asked.

"You bet. Come with me."

It didn't take Nancy long to conclude that what she saw on the monitor was a professional in action. It disappeared before her eyes and Ike handed over a copy. "There you go. I'm calling the cops."

"Thanks, Ike. This stays between me and you, okay?"

"No problem, Nancy. Any time."

Nancy returned to the car and Luz. She replaced her handgun in her bag.

Luz knew her cover was blown.

She reached into Nancy's bag and retrieved a Ruger LC9S. She dropped the magazine and slipped the action. A round popped out. A hand flicked and she caught it.

"This is nice and compact. What backup is in your blouse?"

Nancy pulled out a second magazine.

"Of course."

Luz slipped the round into the magazine and re-inserted it into the butt. She didn't slide the action to put one in the chamber. Instead, she replaced it in Nancy's bag.

"This is between you and me, Luz. Don doesn't need to know. Neither does Tricia, okay?"

"No hay problema, señora. Entiendo. I understand."

But it was a problem for her. A huge problem. Her cover was blown. Perhaps not in a huge way. Still, Nancy wasn't stupid.

Luz could handle herself. And she was knowledgeable about guns. She couldn't do anything about any of it.

"Thank you for looking out my daughter, Luz."

"Of course. I would do nothing less. I love her like my sister."

Nancy reached for Luz's hand and squeezed it with gratitude. It was likely a miracle that the robber was still alive.

"Your dress is ripped, dear."

Luz looked down at her dress for the first time since the assault. It was torn. Tears rolled down her cheeks. "It is ruined now. It was my mother's—"

"I know, Luz. If you let me—"

"No one can fix it. Now everything is gone. Everything."

She silently cursed her predicament brought on by the drug cartels in her country. They had taken it and squeezed every last peso out of it. Murdered entire families. Corrupted every politician, whether local or state or federal. Paid bribes to police and the army. Nothing was off-limits.

"I will start looking for my own place tomorrow," she said.

Chapter 20

Don and Tricia and Lola were waiting on the front steps for the women. He had quizzed his daughter about what happened. She wasn't sure, but she did what Luz told her to do and ran home immediately.

The car turned into the driveway and he heaved a sigh of relief. He didn't doubt his wife's abilities. He knew her too well. Still, he worried occasionally. This was one of those times.

Tricia ran down the steps to greet her mother. "We were worried about you, mom."

She looked at her husband and nodded.

Don acknowledged the look with a grim smile. "I take it that it's handled?"

"It is. You can relax. There won't be any blowback. Luz did an admirable job and Ike is grateful for her help."

"Recordings?"

"None. Problems with the security system."

She revealed the USB stick in her hand and held it up. Don nodded again and marveled at how his wife knew how to handle such things.

Her former job came in handy. Whatever that was. She wouldn't tell him. And she swore him to secrecy if he ever learned about it.

"All right then, folks. While you two were lollygagging about, Trish and I made us dessert. Who wants ice cream cake?"

Nancy looked at Luz and shook her head. "You see what we have to deal with? We have tons of home-cooked food and he takes my daughter out and buys a cake. Men."

Luz rushed past everyone and made for her room.

"What is it with Luz, dear?"

"It's the dress. I was her mother's. It was the last thing she had of her family. It got torn up in the scuffle. I think I can get it fixed for her, but she doesn't want to listen right now."

L uz took off her mother's dress and examined it. It was torn in places. Seams were ripped. It would be impossible for her to repair. She dressed and took it upstairs. She held it up for one last look before gathering it up and putting it in the garbage.

"Luz. Why are you throwing out your dress?"

She turned. Tricia was in the doorway, watching.

"It is ruined. Just like my country and my family are ruined. There is nothing left. I have nothing left. Nada."

"I think my mom could fix it. She likes to sew things. She used to make me skirts and blouses and things."

Luz patted the girl on her shoulder. "It doesn't matter any more, manita." Luz pulled her close and hugged the girl. "It is all right. I will get over it. Lola will help me. You will, too."

Tricia smiled and rushed to her mother. "Luz threw her dress out," she announced. "She called me manita. What's that?"

"It means little sister. And don't worry about her dress. I'll rescue it. But don't tell her. It will be our secret and our surprise, okay?"

Secretly pleased that Luz called her sister, Tricia hurried to the kitchen and the rattling dishes. It still smelled good from the food everyone helped prepare earlier. \
She helped Luz clean the plates.

Don, no stranger to being nagged by his wife, showed up to help.

"Usually, my dad has to be asked to come and help," Tricia said.

Don tut-tutted and rolled up his sleeves. "I most certainly do not."

Luz laughed. "He is like my father. He would come to help too, but he enjoyed more the eating than the cleaning up."

Nancy called from the living room. "I'm going out for a bit. I'll be back shortly."

She folded Luz's dress and placed it in her bag. She grabbed the keys, and she was off to make for her dry cleaners. She held the dress up to show how pretty it was, then laid it on the counter to show him the damage.

"Can you repair it? I can do some, but I'm

no expert, Juan. The materials and the colors—"

"No problemo, Nancy. I will talk to some people I know. Some of the material is special. I think we can do it. It will take some time."

"Time is not a problem. If you have questions, call me, and I will come down. Understand?

"Oh yes. I understand. The dress is special. I knew that the instant I saw it. Do not worry. It will be just the way it was for the lucky person.

"Thank you, Juan. It means a lot to me."

Luz knew her days in the Boyle home were numbered. The way she had dealt with the thief in the store. Handling Nancy's handgun like a professional. Both were mistakes. Both were necessary. Still, it was time to move on. Time to do what she set out to do.

She took out the list of names and then put it away. She knew them by heart. She opened the creased list again. It had traveled with her all those years in Mexico. Across the Caribbean. Into Florida. She took a pen and drew a line after the last name. She wrote a new one beneath.

Santiago.

It was because of him, all those years ago, that she believed anything could be possible. That he had left her with some money to help her made all the difference. She turned into everything she hated. Went to work for the cartels. Got to know their methods and their madness, for there was no method to their madness. That became more and more claro—more clear—the longer she remained in their employ.

But no more. It had been long enough. Terminado. She was done. There would be no more waiting.

She would clean up her cartel enemies the only way she knew how. She would extract payment for the sins the cartels had committed against her family and against her.

She would give no quarter.

Chapter 21

Tricia climbed the darkened stairs from the basement up to her mother's bedroom. She knocked on the door and called out before entering. "Mom? Mom."

She nudged her mother in the dark bedroom. Her father grunted. "What is it, dear?"

"Luz is downstairs crying," Tricia said.

"Are you sure?"

"Yes. I'm sure," she told her mother. "I went to listen. I sent Lola to her."

"Bring her here, dear. Don—"

Don knew the drill. He rolled out of bed. "I'll be downstairs if you need me." He grabbed a pillow and sheets and a blanket from the hall closet and made his way to the living room where he made up the sofa.

Tricia arrived in her mother's bedroom, holding Luz's hand in hers.

"Come on, you two. There's room. Where's Lola?" Nancy asked.

The dog let out a gentle woof and settled in at the foot of the bed.

"I swear, that dog is more human than humans."

Luz made the decision overnight.

She eased out of bed early. She checked the even breathing of the two she was about to leave behind. Even Lola was undisturbed by her movements.

She slipped past Don, still asleep on the living-room sofa, on her way to the basement.

Ever neat and orderly, she hurriedly folded her clothes and placed them in her well-used backpack with her other belongings.

She left a note. She made sure it was purposely brief and vague, careful to let them know she was off to find a place of her own.

Tricia wasn't happy when she discovered her new friend had moved out. She had developed quite a friendship with Luz.

Even Lola roamed the house, listless and snuffling with nose to ground dedicated to searching for her missing human friend.

Nancy sought to reassure her daughter. "I know you miss her, dear. Don't worry. She'll be back when she learns we had her mother's beautiful dress repaired and ready for her."

Days later, Luz called to announce she had found a place. She explained she was busy furnishing it. When it was livable, she would invite everyone over for a Mexican feast.

She never called again.

Luz moved into a small studio in a new multi-story apartment building. It would allow her to be invisible. It had all the usual amenities if she wanted to use them, including a gym and a pool.

She paid cash up front for six months. She slid the envelope across the rental agent's desk. It disappeared, and there were no further questions. She wondered if she was even placed on the resident list. She checked the ground-floor tenant listing and discovered her name wasn't there.

She rented a small van and roamed the second-hand stores. She picked up a table and a chair for the dining room. She found a foam mattress for the floor in the bedroom. She picked out a comfortable chair to relax in for the living room. A small desk and an office chair would do for her research. Two stand-up lamps would be enough for all the light she needed. She found a lounger for the balcony when she wanted her privacy, yet still wanted some fresh air and sunshine.

The building's midtown location was perfect. There was a grocery store nearby. Plenty of public transit bus stops. There were restaurants, too, and fast-food outlets. If she was careful, she would never have to visit the same place twice but for groceries.

She changed her mind about that when she discovered the help wanted sign in the grocery store window. She walked in, asked for an application, and filled it out on the spot. The manager, ever needing workers, glanced briefly at the application, longer at her, and hired her immediately.

She was a local now. Anonymous. Just another worker bee, but for the place where she lived. It was pricey. No one needed to know. She doubted if any of her fellow employees lived in the neighborhood. No one would see her. And if they did—

Luz missed the Boyles, and she missed Tricia and Lola even more. Nancy did so much for her. She owed them all. They were good people.

But that was over. Done with. She was on her own. She had to make her own way, by her own rules, just as she did in Mexico.

She slid the balcony door open. A light breeze drifted in, gently disturbing the sheer curtains. A corner of the paper map on her small dining room table fluttered.

She would pick up a tablet later for a more detailed overhead view.

She slid a chair up to the telescope. It was a last-minute purchase, but she found it extremely useful. She sighted in and focused.

Everything she needed was in front of her, revealed in all its glory. She shifted her head from the eyepiece and looked across at what she knew to be Biscayne Bay. High rise after high rise confronted her. She returned her eye to the high-powered telescope and swung it from side to side, halting at the various buildings. There were almost too many to count.

Her business was there. All her business was there.

And she had all the time in the world to make it her business.

Chapter 22

Luz **consulted the mapping** software a final time. She didn't need to, but the routine was normal for her, and she liked routine. The image was burned into her memory. What threw her off was the enormous yacht moored to the dock.

Could they be that obvious?

Apparently, the answer was yes.

She discovered the small park on one of her forays into the neighborhood. It showed up on the map, but until she saw it for herself, she wasn't certain.

It proved to be perfect. She returned so many times she worried she could be recognized, even with the multitude of disguises she used.

She made sure to arrive and leave at different times. Sometimes she walked. Sometimes she biked. Sometimes she taxied, being sure to get out blocks away

The fancy yacht wasn't an anomaly she had spotted on the computer map. It appeared to be moored permanently. If it ever went to sea, and she didn't witness it leave even once, it always returned.

The only thing she brought with her on her visits to the park were the small binoculars. Even then, she made certain to use them only when she was certain she was alone. When no one watched her. Or checked her out. Sometimes men would approach when she made herself look more presentable as a younger woman. She nodded them off with a determined shake of her head, and eventually they gave up. Possibly she became known as a regular. In fact, she was certain, with each of her disguises.

She overheard a dog over the wall. Children playing and splashing in a pool.

The wife—she assumed it was the wife from the photos she took—sometimes met a lover on board the yacht. He was young and tanned. Perhaps a golf pro from one of the many courses. Each time, he would paddle a kayak to the rendezvous. He silently tied off and climbed aboard the luxurious yacht. It was so huge it didn't even rock when he boarded.

She laughed at her joke and wondered where the husband and his bodyguards were during those times. Perhaps out playing golf, thus the young pro would know when to come and go.

Trees behind the recreation center provided some cover.

The wall around the property presented no obstacle. It was low, only to prevent curious children from dipping fingers and toes into the channel. She was sure she could access the channel from there. Store her gear. Return to pick up her dry getaway clothes.

She wandered into the rec center's

restrooms. Checked the ceilings for loose tiles. She could store a backup with a couple of magazines if it was necessary. She moved to dismiss the idea out of hand and changed her mind in the same instant. Why not? Better safe than sorry.

Would she use the rental? A bicycle? Perhaps the bicycle. Yes. She could transport it on a mount on the back of the rental. She would have to lock it, but that was no obstacle. A magnetic key holder would make sure.

One problem presented itself, though. The park closed at dusk. The parking lot was still accessible, of course. How much of a problem would that be? Would curious neighbors complain? Would the police arrive?

She tested and tested again. Nothing. Not even a curious passer-by paid attention or stopped.

Satisfied with the unanticipated antics of the wife on the yacht, she moved on to the husband. She used the bicycle to pedal past the entrance to the house.

Faked a flattening tire and pretended to pump it up.

Wiped sweat from her forehead in the humid city air.

She followed her target to his golf course of choice.

She was right about the bodyguards. They would load up rented clubs in two carts and accompany their boss. If it was hot, they played nine. If it was cool, they played 18. Only occasionally did they stop at the clubhouse for food or drink.

She had to know. Was the SUV armored? In the golf course parking lot, she bumped it with her rental. It shifted. Rocked. She got out to inspect the damage. Of course there was none, but she needed to see the windows close up. If she was lucky—

And she was. No armored glass. Which meant the SUV was standard off the lot. Still, she would need something more powerful than her .22 to break the glass. Not a problem. She would have it.

A dilemma presented itself.

Would she chase them all the way back to the house? Wait for the gate to open. Pursue the SUV on foot past the open gate. Hit them as the gate closed. Proceed to the house and clean up the rest.

From there she would swim across the channel to retrieve her gear.

But not before taking care of the wife and her lover.

The yacht wouldn't be a problem. She destroyed more than a few when she was younger.

Santiago. El salvador. Her savior. She smiled, remembering how James stashed money in one of her bags. A tear slipped down her cheek at the memory of discovering the cash. She swiped it away. She recalled the go-fast she blew up. Making her way ashore with Jim's money and the clothes Anya had left for her.

It was so long ago. Her life since then would not make her Santiago very happy.

She shook it all off and launched the tiny drone. It was almost silent. She guided it across the water. Made sure her phone was set to record. She kept the drone off the property. High enough that she could see everything she needed to see.

On its return flight, she killed the motors. She had no further use for it. It plopped into the Biscayne Waterway, causing ripples like a fish jumping.

L uz made her way home, stopping on the way for takeout. Her night would be a busy one reviewing the drone footage. She had to be sure the cover was staked out if things went sideways.

Dedication to duty. As a highly paid sicaria, it was one thing she was noted for.

Well, they were about to find out how dedicated she was.

She pored over the footage on her tablet. The resolution provided by the tiny drone was remarkable. She marveled as she checked trees and planters and shrubbery. Calculated distances. Figured sight lines. Looked for automatic lights and camera mounts. For those the drone video missed, she looked to more sight lines from the occupant's point of view.

Even with the careful planning that went into all of her jobs, she was always nervous putting in the work to make each job successful. Had anyone seen her? Anyone who might recognize her? Did the drone make so much noise it was noticed? What about the splash in the water? Was there a flash of reflected light from the binoculars?

She referred to her notebook often. Those small black hardback notebooks were perfect for her needs. She had it all down. Sketches from the drone footage. Days when wife met lover on board the yacht. Learned it was when husband spent time on the golf course. Which was quite often.

All noted and checked and double-checked and reviewed and memorized.

When she finished with her recons, when she had everything tied up in one neat package, she would make her move. There was no rush. These people were refugees from the disaster occurring in Mexico. Family. Moved out and secreted away. To be protected from people like her who would be bent on revenge.

So they thought.

Up to now.

If she planned well. Thought things through. Exercised her experience. Made use of what she learned over the course of years. With planning, luck and good fortune, she might get two, maybe three.

Before word got out.

Chapter 23

Nancy Boyle was no longer so certain about Luz. What was nagging at her came to the fore following the aborted corner store robbery and how Luz had secured the scene. Unarmed and single-handed, Luz disarmed a robber intent on mayhem. That she had the sense to instruct Tricia to run home with Lola beforehand endeared the woman to her. How she handled her pistol in the car afterwards hinted Luz was not one to be trifled with.

She knew. She had experience with such things.

Which was all the more reason to cause her to wonder what happened to the girl. Luz told them she would call when she found a place. That she would invite all of them over for a Mexican feast.

It never happened.

Thus it was that Nancy pulled out the list she found and copied when she went through Luz's backpack following the store incident. Creased and faded, the list was ragged from folding and unfolding. Obviously, it was with the girl for a long time.

One entry at the bottom stood out. It was

more recent, as evidenced by the fresh ink.

She had photographed the list and put it back where she found it.

She brought it up on her phone now. Sent it to the printer in the small home office. Once in her hands, she took another look. A very young girl's careful print script. Written with care and dedication. She recognized the loving nicknames for Mother and Father and Sister and Brother. Even a dog's name.

There were given names beneath the first entry, that of Mother. She didn't recognize any of them. Why would she? There were other names beneath each of the family members as well. However, it was the last name on the list that had her concerned.

Santiago.

It was what she heard Luz call Jim.

The five at the top of the list were a series of names. Obviously all first names. Or at least, no last names she recognized. Commas separated the names on each line. Were they families? Partners? Business associates?

She folded the list and placed it in her sewing drawer, and wondered if she should show Jim. It was obvious he was a part of it. For good, or for bad? That was what she didn't know.

She decided to wait. There was no sense upsetting anyone over a simple list of names. She'd talk it over with Maddie the next time she saw her.

Nancy felt a need to retrieve her Ruger from the breadbox. She unfolded a dish towel and placed it on the table. Pulled the magazine and placed the handgun on the kitchen table on the towel. She closed her eyes and stripped it. When she finished, she kept her eyes closed and re-assembled the handgun. Satisfied, she returned the handgun to the bread box. It was a small thing, but it comforted her to know she could do it.

"Are you expecting trouble?"

Don's voice startled her concentration momentarily.

"No. I don't think so."

She went to the office to retrieve the list. "Look at this."

Don contemplated it before responding. "Is someone picking names for a baby? A Mexican baby? There are more than a few Spanish names there."

Nancy took another look. "You're right. I should have noticed that. You could be right, though. Names for a new member of the family, perhaps."

She considered mentioning something about Santiago on the bottom.

"That's funny," Don said.

She looked up at her husband. "What's funny, dear?"

"Santiago." He said the name slowly, as though remembering.

"What about it?"

"It's what I overheard Luz call Jim. When she recognized him in the diner."

Chapter 24

Luz almost didn't see him. When she noticed, she cursed her own stupidity.

"Madre mía."

He fit in almost as good as she did.

She cursed again for being such a slacker.

Of course they would have a cartel spotter. More than one, even. It's what they did. They covered all the bases. And then some. It was what had made her so proficient at what she did. She rounded the bases every time for a home run. She smiled to herself for making the baseball connection. She was in America only a short while and already she was using sports metaphors in her speech.

The smile disappeared instantly when she recognized him in a storefront reflection. If it had been daytime—

It was the second time. And he was matching her pace on the bicycle. He was good, too. Not as good as she was. But good enough that she hadn't noticed him right off.

The diversion came up on her. Unexpected. She braked rapidly and turned toward it. Stopped. Leaned the bike on its stand. Looked in the window, using her hands to catch the reflection. He was cycling past her. Then he, too, turned and pedaled in her direction. Coasted to a stop beside her.

She tensed. Anticipated.

She spoke first. "I didn't know this place was here." Nonchalant.

Even so, he was too close. He stayed bent over the handlebars. She wondered if he knew. She could kill him where he stopped. A single strike to the throat would do it. It wouldn't even be a challenge.

"I didn't know either." The teenager's eyes shifted to her bike. It was no surprise. She determinedly kept it bare bones. It was rusted from the salt air when she bought it. Never washed or polished. It was a junker. To keep anyone from stealing it. Or noticing it.

"Are you looking for an upgrade?"

She threw him a look. Insulted.

"No. Do you think I should?"

He held up his hands. "I didn't mean anything. You can ride whatever you want. Maybe—"

She looked at the reflection in the window. He appeared innocent enough now. Maybe too innocent, but still. She was beginning to think he didn't know. That he was only looking for a date. It happened sometimes. Not often.

"Yes?"

"Maybe we could meet here when it's open. You know, to check out the newer models. Get a coffee next door. If you want."

She didn't want. But she had to know. "All right. When?"

"Do you work?" Alarms started to go off again.

"No. Not yet. I'm still looking for work. You?" she wondered.

"Me neither," the teenager said. "I'm looking, too."

That didn't satisfy her.

"All right then. It's a date."

Luz regretted the words. They slipped out too fast. "I mean—"

He interrupted. "No problemo."

His eyes wandered to the sign. "They open at 10. How about at 11?"

It would be close. She had a shift at the grocery store. It began at noon. She wouldn't be on time. "Ten would be better," she told him.

"You're an early bird," he said. "I like that. I'll see you then."

She waited for him to ride off. Circled the block at speed. Hoped she would catch him, unaware she had reversed his play. She switched off her lights. Caught sight of a blinking red light. Chased after it and knew she had him.

It took her ten blocks—or was it 15— before he turned into a driveway. An older house. She waited before approaching. Pulled out her phone and snapped a picture in the dark.

Luz knew then she definitely dumped the drone into the water too soon. She made a note to pick up another before pedaling off into the night. She stopped half a dozen times to check for a tail. Didn't see one. Either he was that good, or she was better.

She hoped it was the latter. She didn't make for home right off. Instead, she stopped for some Chinese. Lingered in a corner of the restaurant. Checked and double checked.

She stopped one last time at a food truck. Ordered a drink. Lingered some more with eyes wide open.

By the time she arrived home, she was exhausted. There was no time for sleep. She opened her laptop and pulled up the mapping software. She typed in the address of the safe house—she was already calling it that in her mind—and zoomed down on it.

It was typical for the neighborhood. Nothing special. A two-car garage. A shed.

Her night wasn't over. Immediately, she made for the bathroom and donned a gray wig. Aged her face with makeup. Put on the special knee brace she adjusted to cause her to limp. Picked up the cane.

In ten minutes, she pulled out of the underground parking.

Chapter 25

Luz **parked the car.**
Pulled the jet-black hoodie over the grannie wig.

She opened the door and got out. No interior light switched on.

She popped the trunk and pulled on the second skin of snug-fitting leather gloves. Opened her backpack. By feel she found and checked the action on the .22 Long Rifle pistol. Wrapped a home-made Velcro belt around her waist and snugged it to carry her backup magazines.

Satisfied, she eased the trunk closed and looked around.

The neighborhood windows appeared to be dark. A senior citizen neighborhood, she called them.

She made her way to the safe house. No gate. Garage closed. Around the side, she located a side door. Took her time jimmying the lock. She knew the door into the house from the garage would be unlocked. Most were even in the better neighborhoods back in Mexico.

Except she wasn't in Mexico. The country

was no longer her home. She had burned all of her bridges and committed to moving on.

She opened the garage door's side entrance and entered the garage, careful to leave it unlatched behind her.

She listened for the sound of a television or a radio or music. Proceeded to the house door. Tested it. She was right. It, too, was unlocked. She eased it open to reveal a faint light in the kitchen.

Night lights. Unfamiliar. Not the kind she was accustomed to. These gave off a very faint green tinge. Were they something special? Help for night vision goggles? There was no time to evaluate.

Luz made her way into the kitchen. Surprised a man behind a fridge door. Fired twice. He dropped with a hard thump. The fridge door remained open. A second man at the table stood up. Went for his weapon.

Unrelenting, she advanced.

He wasn't expecting her to keep advancing. She ignored the startled look on his face and fired two more times. He settled back in his chair and collapsed over the table. Dishes rattled.

She waited. No one came.

She dropped a magazine and reloaded. She preferred to work with full mags. She picked up the dropped magazine and replaced it on her belt.

She stepped over the bodies and headed down the hall to a bedroom. More green light. She fired four times into the bed. Pulled back the sheet and fired twice. That was number three.

She dropped the magazine and reloaded the Model 71 small-calibre automatic.

She knew better than to show up like this. Without doing a recon. She didn't even know if these men were cartel spotters. She didn't know what they were. For all she knew—

She stopped thinking.

Where was number four? Where was her bicycle-riding companion? He had to be somewhere. There was been too much noise for him not to know something was going on.

She opened another bedroom door. Entered and pulled down a sheet. Nothing. She advanced down the hall. Found the last bedroom. It too was empty. She made to fire into the bed and changed her mind.

She heard the noise behind her too late.

The garrote tightened around her neck.

She snaked fingers through. Barely protected her throat from its tightening. The rubber glove over her leather glove melted with the pressure.

It had to be bike rider. He was the same size as her. He had the advantage of surprise.

He lost the advantage the instant he allowed her to bend.

She dropped the automatic and went for the knife in her boot. Desperate, she jerked it out. Ran the razor-sharp blade up the inside of her attacker's opposite leg. He screamed. His grip on the garrote loosened only a little.

She knew too that it would soon lock in.

She thrust again with the knife. It went deep into his thigh and struck bone. He screamed again. She straightened. The movement threw him off balance.

It was her chance.

She fell back.

Twisted.

Went for her second blade and jabbed up and into his rib cage.

She saw recognition in his eyes as he bled out.

She retrieved the Model 71, leveled it, and gave him two in the forehead. It was the only way she knew to guarantee the kill.

Luz went from room to room, checking for her dropped magazines. She wasn't concerned with the shell casings of the small-caliber weapon.

She checked the faces of the men. Three Mexican. One norte americano—she recognized her bike-riding friend.

She didn't waste time wondering why he was doing what he did. Drug money bought him. Drug money killed him.

Just like it had killed her family.

She left the house the same way she entered and limped her way to the car.

The houses were still dark. Luz thanked the quiet Model 71 for that.

A long time ago she learned she must always be prepared.

She arrived at her car and opened the trunk. She quickly reloaded the spent magazines in her belt and pistol before replacing them in the backpack.

She had a decision to make, and she had to make it fast.

Chapter 26

Don **Boyle's unmarked police** vehicle screamed past a black and white with lights flashing. Another blocked access farther down the street.

Plain clothes officers armed with AR-15s patrolled. They gathered behind Don as he approached his house.

Emma Mayberry, on lookout from the front window, witnessed the arrival of Don and his crew. She unlocked the front door and opened it wide to allow the men to enter.

Don's wife, Nancy, introduced Emma Mayberry while explaining she was helping out for the moment.

An officers noticed the bulge under Emma's shirt. "What are you carrying, miss?"

Emma looked to Don. He barely nodded. She pulled up her shirt to reveal the handgun.

The questioning continued. "Have you got a license for that?".

"Of course I do, officer. I'm also a licensed Private Investigator. Would you like to see the paper?"

"That won't be necessary for now," he said.

Meanwhile, Nancy was frantically whispering to Don.

Emma was pretty sure Nancy was explaining the MP5 hanging off her right shoulder. It was concealed by the huge shirt she was wearing. The firearm was a marvel of German gun engineering and manufacturing. Compact. Light. With an effective suppressor. Sadly, it wasn't legal in the form she was carrying. And she knew the question was coming.

The cop turned away, changed his mind and looked at Emma again. "What have you got on the other side, miss?"

Emma's eyes shifted to Don. He shook his head from side to side ever so slightly.

"Oh, that rusty old thing is a double-barreled sawed-off." She reached into a pocket and pulled out a couple of shotgun shells. "This is my backup magazine." She smiled at the officer.

Don stepped in to quell further questions and discussion. "Officers, I think we could use you and your firepower out at your vehicles. I'll put on some coffee and I think the wife has fresh-made donuts. How does that sound?"

The grumbling ceased, and in five minutes the men left the house carrying coffee and home-made donuts.

"Now then, where are my daughter and my dog? But mostly my daughter," Don asked his wife.

It was Emma who stepped up to answer. "Jim and Maddie have Tricia. They're taking her to a safe location at a marina. I know the people and I'm familiar with the place. It's safe. It's a long car ride, but it's necessary. Maddie and the dogs are going to stay with Tricia in a trailer. Jim will come back if you need him."

Don looked at his wife. "I think I'd like him to stay there if that's all right. What do you think, Nancy?" he asked.

Don's wife nodded assent.

Emma got on the phone immediately. When she hung up, the arrangement was made to have Jim remain behind at the marina.

Don turned to Emma. "One more thing. What's really hanging off your right side?"

Emma unbuttoned her shirt and removed it, revealing the suppressed MP5. She turned, revealing the illegal 30-shot magazines for her Model17 across her back. A second rail for the MP5 was strapped to her front.

"That's quite the shotgun you have there. You better keep it covered up. You've got more and better firepower than my friends in the street."

Emma moved to button her Hawaiian shirt.

"You're also forgiven for setting fire to that armored van and walking away with that unknown black dog," Don added with a smile.

Emma returned the smile. "I don't know what you're talking about, officer. I'm sure I've never driven an armored vehicle in my life."

Nancy shook her head. "All right, you two. I suspect there's a story there, but I think I'm going to have to get Jim to tell it. Who wants some of my coffee and home-made donuts?"

"First things first, dear wife," Don said. "When and if the action starts, I'll take the front. Emma will take the back. You, my dear, will hold the center. If need be, that's where we will retreat and hold out. Understood?"

With unanimous consent, the trio made for the kitchen and the treats.

Nancy loaded a second tray and went off to refresh and refill the officers in the street. She was forced to listen to a chorus of, 'Thank you Mrs. Boyle. Don is a lucky man', before she could break free and return to her house.

Nancy still wasn't certain what caused the commotion. Don hadn't taken the time to explain. All she knew was that she had to get Tricia, their daughter, out of town. That was when she had tasked Jim and Maddie with the task. "Are you going to tell me what's going on, Donald Boyle? I'm sure Emma would like to know, too."

Don sat down at the table with his coffee and a donut. "First things first, dear." He grinned across the table at Emma and his wife. The grin soon disappeared. "I have it on good authority—authority being informants—that there's a crew of ex-cons who took exception to my being responsible for their incarceration. They're fortunate enough to be out on parole, but that doesn't appear to be adequate for their simple minds. They want to even the score, so to speak."

"How many?" Emma asked, wanting to know what she was up against.

Don held up his hand. "Apparently, they're

well-armed and waiting for the perfect opportunity, whatever that is. I heard some grumblings only this morning that it could be today." He went on. "To answer your question, Emma, it could be three. No more, according to my informant."

Emma said, "What do you think of doing a back-yard sweep? Your yard has a lot of shrubbery ideal for concealment."

"Not a bad idea. Let's do it together. Nancy, would you mind holding down the home front while Emma and I do the investigating?" He grinned at the two women. "Do you see what I did there?"

"Donald, we get it. Now do your duty. Emma, be grateful you don't have to put up with this man's sense of humor on a regular basis."

"Oh, believe me, I am. I think I might just take a course in armored vehicle driving to put home a point."

Chapter 27

Nancy barely got the front door closed. Screeching tires and AR-15 fire caused her to hurry into the living room. She began forcing the furniture into a protective circle. Metal banged into metal and the gunfire halted.

Don's Rover chirped and a disembodied voice listed the body count. "One down. We're all good in front."

Emma's suppressed weapon barked quietly. She fired in bursts of five, again and again. Don rushed to her side by the back door. "That's not a standard MP5."

"No. Jim had them modified."

She talked between bursts. "Single fire." She made the change instantly. "Three-burst." Another instant change and she let go with a three-round burst. "And finally, a five-burst. For when you want a little more, but full auto would burn up too much ammo. I really like the 3-burst. Five is just okay. It does full auto, too. Didn't I say that already?"

Emma halted frequently while she talked up the usefulness of the MP5. "It conserves ammo and makes the dual rails last like forever. It's also pretty accurate if you take your time."

She let off with another quick burst. "Short range, of course. I don't think those so-called friends of yours had any idea what they were going to be up against."

The pinging inside the house quieted. Emma held up a hand. "Do we want to do a body count?"

Don called to his wife, hunkered down in the living room. "Firing has gone quiet. We're going out to get a count. Are you okay in there?"

"I'm good. I'll stay here, thank you very much," Nancy called out.

"No problem. We can handle it. I think Emma evened the score, if there ever was one to be evened."

He spoke confidently to Emma. "Let's go."

"Not so fast, copper. First things first."

Emma broke out a fresh rail and inserted one side of the dual magazine into the MP5.

"Is that only your second?" Don asked, incredulous.

"It makes for a good fit with the three-burst. Or the five. And yes. Now let's go check the damages."

Emma changed her mind as sirens wailed in the background. "I think we know what's coming. Your friends out front must have called in help. I'm going to police my brass so we don't get caught up where we don't want to be. Where should I stash this?" Emma unhooked the MP5 from her shoulder strap.

"Ask Nancy if you can put it under our mattress for now, okay? She'll know why."

Emma witnessed Nancy sweeping up the brass in the kitchen. "Thanks. I was wondering how I'd get rid of that with those sirens getting louder. Uhh, Don—" she hesitated.

"Bedroom is down the hall on your right. Beneath the mattress should be fine. You better add Jim's mags and the rest of it to the mix."

Emma rushed to complete stashing the weaponry before SWAT arrived.

Nancy called from the kitchen doorway while she busied herself sweeping the floor.

"When you're done, bacon is frying. Coffee is ready. Check the eggs. I'll make toast. We're going to have quite a crowd here. Let's see how professional they can be once they get a smell of the goodies."

Nancy smiled sweetly in Don's direction.

Don's Rover crackled with information on SWAT's ETA.

"Come on, ladies. We need to get out in the front yard. I'll hold up my badge. You both need to remain behind me and a bit off to the side so they can see you. No matter what. Understood? Hold up your arms like I do."

The women acknowledged his instructions.

"Emma. Where's your sidearm? You need to make it disappear," Don said.

"It's under your bed with everything else, if you get my drift," she told him.

"Good. Now let's go. We don't want to

keep SWAT waiting."

On the Boyle lawn, the five badges belonging to Boyle and the four plainclothes officers held up at arm's length confronted the arriving SWAT team. After a cursory inspection, the five were led away for questioning. Emma and Nancy were permitted to enter the house. They busied themselves setting out plates and cutlery and filling coffee cups and dishing out donuts.

"When did you get the donuts, Nancy?" Emma wanted to know.

"It's an old trick I learned years ago when I first met Don. A cop never travels so far that he doesn't know where the nearest donut shop is. I started making them at home so he knew where to come."

"Emma laughed, and Nancy joined her." "Do you want to call Maddie and let her know we're all okay?"

"No, dear. I don't need to know where they are," Nancy told her. "You do it. Next time and all that."

Emma put through the call and explained their situation as under control. That so far, it looked like it was one of Don's old arrests and any friends the man had been able to convince to ride along to take revenge. "The coast is clear for a return any time," she told Maddie.

She listened while Maddie explained that Tricia and Lola were none the worse for wear. Both she and Lola were getting some training in dog handling from an expert. They'd be taking a few extra days, if it was all right with

Nancy and Don. As it turned out, it was, and everyone was happy.

"Don will be busy patching up the house, anyway. He doesn't need either of them helping. Even Jim, if you get my drift," Nancy said.

It was settled, and Emma hung up. Don cleared away the SWAT and the detectives come to investigate and interview. He settled into a chair at the kitchen table across from Emma.

"So, Emma. Tell me how you met Maddie and Jim."

Emma was unprepared for the straightforward question. She was expecting more from Don over the burning van she and Friday had abandoned during their last escapade together.

"There's not much to tell. The three of them were headed by car from Denver to Vail on a ski holiday. They got stranded in a blizzard and took shelter in the small town where I lived. Their dog—Friday—turned out to be quite a character."

"How so?"

"From what they told me, every time he stuck his bum in the snow to do his business, he'd rush back into the hotel room and chase anyone still in a warm bed out of it with his cold nose. I think that's the reason why Jim and Friday snooze in the office sunbeam so often." She giggled at the picture and settled back in her chair.

"There was a small matter of some bank

robbers taking us all hostage," she added, "but good boy Friday saved the day there, too. Well, he did after I used the snow plow to chase down one of the robbers."

Nancy looked across the table at Emma. "You know how to drive one of those huge plows?"

"I do. It was my dad's job. He used to let me sit in his lap when I was a little girl, so I come by it naturally. Anyway, that's about it. It gets boring after that. I came to Florida for my paramedic training. Jim and Maddie offered me a place to stay until I graduated. I couldn't refuse the rent, and the rest is history."

"Well, Don and I thank you for standing by us. You certainly didn't have to."

"It's not a problem. I like to help when I can. They'd do the same for me."

Emma didn't mention they already had.

Chapter 28

Luz eased the trunk closed. She used her weight to secure it with a quiet click. She cursed silently when she was forced to open it again to unload her folding bicycle.

She cursed a second time when she remembered to switch out the 71 with the older Model 70. She never used the same weapon on multiple hits on the same day.

She zipped her backpack and slid it over her shouters, leaving the trunk empty.

Mistakes. She was making mistakes. Mistakes that could get her killed. Time was running out. She was behind. All because she made the rash decision to hit the safe house on account of one americano spotter. Who had the temerity to ask her on a date as a cover for tailing her.

He wouldn't be following her any longer. But thanks to him and time wasted, she had a dilemma. Already there was a dim gray light in the east. She would have to pedal her ass off.

Luz tightened the straps on her backpack. Fastened the cross hitch. Pulled on her thin leather gloves. Tested her reach for the various pockets depending on the tools she would need. The most important, the magazines. She checked again. They were within easy reach. She bent and checked her multiple boot knives. She made sure both lights on the bike were out.

She was good to go. Still, she was reluctant. She had no plan for the sudden change to her well thought out first plan.

No matter. She had to do it. The writing was done and over with. What was the English expression? The writing on the wall, or something. She shrugged and threw a leg over the bike. Looked to the eastern horizon. In at most twenty minutes, she would be out of time.

Traffic was minimal. She blew through the intersections. Ran all the lights because the bike was quiet and she could hear the cars coming.

She made the neighborhood in record time, sweating and huffing as she braked to a halt a block away. She leaned the bike against a fence and proceeded on foot at a fast walk.

In her mind, she pictured the images she had from the drone. Recalled the light stands. Expected they would be automated. She imagined a path between planters and trees and bushes that would provide cover.

Finally, at the gate, she halted. Checked the number pad. It would be useless. She had no code. Perhaps if she had reigned in her excitement at killing the spotters, she might have thought of that. But then, she didn't know she would need a code.

She cursed her stupidity. Of course she would need a code. It was the modern way in this country.

That's how haphazard her current operation was turning out to be. She cursed once more, desperate and determined to carry out the job or die trying. It wouldn't be the first time she made mistakes. No doubt it wouldn't be the last—no matter how hard she tried to eliminate them. And learn from them.

Do or die. She was accustomed to that. So far, it had been only do.

She snugged her gloves and pulled herself up past the edge of the brick wall for a look. No lights came on. She walked to the other side of the gate and did the same. There was nothing.

In Mexico, the top of the wall would have broken glass embedded in the cement. Not here.

Could she be that lucky with the lights? Surely, if there were no infrared, there would be cameras. Of course there would. But it was late. Perhaps coming up to a shift change. The sole guard would be drowsy. Maybe even sleeping. Would he be thinking about his replacement?

She pulled herself over the wall and jumped down into the shadow of darkness. Even with bent knees, she landed with a thud.

The grass was wet from a recent watering.

A dog barked. Ran full bore up to her. Growled. Tried to stop in the wet grass. The dog slid into her. She almost toppled. Regained her balance and reached for a boot knife. The blade flickered as overhead lights flickered.

They didn't stay on. She would replace the shiny knife blades with black metal.

She dispatched the dog with nary a sound. In a single move, she withdrew the slick blade and covered the dulled glint with a hand. She wiped it on the dog's fur and replaced it in her boot.

It wasn't too late.

She could turn around. Climb the wall. Head back to her comfortable apartment. Pretend nothing had happened. Cook Mexican food for her Santiago and Maddie and their friends. Except—

It wasn't about her.

It was about her mother and her father.

It was about her brother and sister and Reynaldo, her cousin.

Even her dog. Her dog had been the last. Even her little Cosa, the last remaining comfort for a little girl, was taken away.

She swore vengeance. And vengeance it would be.

Do or die.

Chapter 29

It **was sometime during** the last two years Luz learned this family moved to Miami. Supposedly to safer ground. The move put them at the top of her list. Her kill list. It was the family of the cartel jefe, or leader, who ordered the death of her entire family.

She had watched the slaughter, concealed from sight in a closet. Holding her little Cosa in her arms.

When she thought back, that alone told her the killers were incompetent. Not right away, of course, but after her training—

She had sneaked outside carrying her teddy bear. Holding Cosa. There was nothing she could do but make a child's promise. She recalled crossing her little fingers. When the time came, if it ever did, she would kill them all for murdering her family.

The time had come. She was resigned, plan or no plan.

Luz crouched and made her way slowly and carefully to the twin palms, her first protected position. Still, there were no lights beyond that first flicker. Surely that wasn't normal.

Shouldn't there be lights coming on?

She advanced to the cement planter and waited. Still nothing. She reached over her shoulder and drew her familiar 70. Her fingers touched her backup weapon, a Model 17. Comforted by its feel, she relaxed only slightly.

She had modified the weapon to provide full automatic mode, and further changed it to do a burst of two shots with a single trigger pull.

A quick burst of two shots was her trademark kill, if it could be called that. It wasn't always. It took her years to develop the skill.

Luz continued her advance toward the side of the house. Either everyone was asleep, including the guard, or a surprise was waiting. Surely they had cameras. Infrared cameras, to be specific. Had the family become so complacent in America that security was now a second thought?

Perhaps it was so. The family had been here for two or perhaps even three years, in relative safety.

She made the side of the house without making a sound. She replaced the smaller automatic in her bag and withdrew the larger handgun. Reached in again and withdrew a suppressor. It took seconds to screw the specially made suppressor onto the automatic's muzzle.

The .22 Long Rifle made little noise.

The Model 17 could be a deal breaker if left unsuppressed.

Luz felt much better with the more powerful automatic. Rather than carry it at her thigh, she gripped it with both hands. It wouldn't matter if anyone recognized it or not.

She was here to kill.

None would remain to tell the tale.

She rounded the corner of the house. A small fire burned in the fire pit. Presumably gas powered, since she hadn't run into a stack of firewood at the side of the house. It told her that someone had been outside recently and might return. She wanted them inside to muffle the sounds of her gunfire.

Wine glasses and plates littered the patio table. A romantic dinner for two, maybe. With the kids in bed. If the husband knew about the lover on the yacht, would the dinner be so romantic?

Where were the guards?

Where were the lights?

Chapter 30

Police Detective Don Boyle didn't usually work a graveyard shift. A couple of sick call-ins forced him to take the late shift. He didn't mind. If it wasn't busy, he would get out of the station to meet up with street cops he hadn't seen in years. It gave him an opportunity to catch up on rumors and lies, as he liked to call them.

When the Rover sparked, he was sitting on a bench enjoying some barbecue at a truck he hadn't visited in years. He acknowledged the call directing him to a house in a neighborhood not far from where he was parked.

He rolled up the foil. He'd have time to enjoy it later.

He lit up the grill lights and slapped a magnetic flasher on the roof before making for the address.

The number of cars on-scene told him he wouldn't be closing out the shift in an hour.

He sent Nancy a quick text advising he wouldn't be home for breakfast before he got out.

He made for the yellow tape. Signed in.

Collected booties and gloves. Walked toward the gate to the yard. Someone had turned on the property's overhead lights.

So, perhaps they came in over the wall. Or through the open gate. Once past the open gate, he looked along both interior walls.

An officer was bent over a dead dog.

He ignored it and advanced to the house.

Former senior partners came to mind when he was a new detective. Despite wearing gloves, he placed his hands in his pockets and made for the interior of the house.

He was confronted by the first of the bodies. Cuban, at first glance. Perhaps Mexican. Two in the forehead. He spotted the brass on the floor. "Is that .22 Long Rifle?"

He bent down for a better look, hands still in pockets. He hadn't seen those at a crime scene, if ever, in his recollection. A target pistol, maybe. Every crime scene he could remember involving firearms had at least a .38 and, more often much larger-caliber weapons these days.

"Yes, it is," one of the men told him. "Exactly two for each body. So far. First glance tells me straight into the forehead of each victim. No brass collected by the look of it. It's still scattered around."

"Interesting."

The first two bodies were almost one on top of the other. It looked as though they couldn't get out of the way fast enough. They dropped where they stood. One right after the other. In very close quarters.

He exited the house and walked over to the

responding officers. "How did the call come in?" he asked.

"A neighbor called in fireworks exploding. Dispatch sent us to investigate. The gate was open. We spotted the open door, and here we are."

"Must have been pretty quiet fireworks by the look of it," Don said.

"How so?"

"Those are .22 Long Rifle. We should probably do some canvassing to see who was awake and who wasn't."

Don turned to go back into the house for a look at the third victim, thinking forensics would be finished with the preliminary.

His Rover barked a second time.

Chapter 31

Nancy **turned off the** television. Something was bothering her about the names of the people that were present in the house. She recognized them as Cuban, only because that was the more common. They could be Mexican. All shot dead. She didn't dwell on the ages. Or the sexes. It had to be over drugs, most definitely.

She went back to the kitchen and her baking. She opened the oven door and closed it immediately.

Something twigged.

She knew right away what that something was.

She went into the office and retrieved the list of names she found in Luz's backpack.

She unfolded the copy and right away, an undeniable fact confronted her.

Every one of the first names in the news report the announcer read out was the same as those that headed up the list. She replaced it and hurried to her phone.

Her first call was to Jim and Maddie. "I need you to get Tricia out of town. Right now."

She was pleased Jim didn't waste her time asking questions. He took her request at face value.

She hung up the phone and called her husband. He didn't pick up. He had to be still working the case he texted her about and couldn't answer.

Jim Nash double-timed it up the stairs to the apartment he shared with Maddie on the third floor. "Nancy needs us to pick up Tricia. Arm up. Now."

Maddie knew better than to ask. The Boyles were personal friends. She liked them a lot. She retrieved the vests and three of the MP5s from the gun safe. They were reserved for what they called special occasions.

She laid the firearms on the kitchen table and rushed down the hall to knock on Emma's door.

"We have to get Tricia out of town. Are you available?"

Emma withdrew from the door. Without saying a word, she opened her own gun safe and retrieved the Model 17 and three of Jim's special magazines, complete with the Velcro strap harness she had jury-rigged. It would allow her to wear the super-long magazines on her back where they would be concealed beneath a shirt.

She rushed down to Jim's office and donned a vest before strapping on her autdomatic and the magazines. She put on a long, loose Hawaiian shirt to cover everything before buttoning it up. "I'm ready," she announced.

One at a time, Emma picked up a dual rail and inserted one of the 30-round magazines. This would allow for a 60-round capability for each of the suppressed weapons. She threw the extra magazines into a bag before donning the weapon's carry-strap over her right shoulder. When she saw what Jim and Maddie had done to conceal their HK firearms, she slipped the right shoulder out of her shirt and did the same.

Maddie called to her dog. "Friday. Come. Car ride."

Together, the three descended the stairs and made for Jim's Packard. He raised the top at the first light. "I don't know what's going on. Nancy called and asked me to pick up Tricia and get her out of town as soon as possible. I didn't ask questions. I have no idea what we'll be facing. Whatever it is, I hope we're ready."

Magazines were released and clicked into the MP5s.

"I don't need to remind you these things aren't legal. I don't think Don will care, but I'm not running any lights to find out if anyone else will, if you get my drift."

Standard magazines slipped in and out of automatics. Maddie checked Jim's. "Yours is good to go. So are the MP5s Emma prepared with the dual rails and suppressors. We have spare vests for Tricia and Nancy. If we need anything else—"

"There's MREs in the trunk. Water too. When we get there, you might want to get some out for us. I guess you know where we'll be taking her."

Maddie only nodded. She opened the dash and took out the new burn phone. "I'll call them."

"I think you better do it from outside the car. Just in case," Jim said.

Maddie snapped the flip phone closed. She didn't want to take a chance on the car being bugged.

Jim pulled into the Boyle yard. He maneuvered the heavy Packard over the finely trimmed green grass of the front lawn and pulled up to the steps. He halted just far enough away to allow the passenger door to open.

Emma got out and walked to the edge of the lawn and the sidewalk. Her eyes roamed the street, first in one direction, and then the other. "Clear!" she announced.

Maddie got out with a vest and climbed the steps to the house. She handed it to Nancy who in turn put it on her daughter. She checked the straps to be sure they were properly attached. A nervous Lola circled the humans, not sure what was happening.

Maddie handed Nancy the second vest, and she donned it. Tricia made for the front door. Her mother called her back. "Not yet, dear. Uncle Jim and Aunt Maddie have to do some things first."

Emma wasn't visible out on the sidewalk. She was busy patrolling the street in front of the house. Jim did the same from the opposite side. If they had to, they would be able to provide crossfire in any direction. The MP5s with their suppressors wouldn't alarm the neighbors.

"Emma is going to stay with you while we move Tricia to a safe house. We'll call when we get there."

"Don't tell me where," she said. I don't need to know.

"No problem. When we get there, I'll stay with her while Jim returns. Is that all right?"

Nancy considered while looking at the huge Packard. She was familiar with it, having driven it several times.

"Don't worry, Nancy. Tricia and Lola will be safe. The back seat is protected by armor plate. The sides have ballistic nylon. The front doors are armored.

"I didn't know that. No wonder the car is so heavy to drive."

"You didn't need to know. Now you do," Maddie told her.

Nancy looked relieved. "Understood and appreciated."

"Friday is going to stay with us. He's capable of helping us if we need it. I don't know about Lola."

Nancy bent to pet the dog. "Lola is just one happy, sloppy family dog, aren't you, Lola?"

The dog nuzzled and licked at her hand and sat down beside Nancy. "See what I mean?"

Satisfied that there were no threats visible, Jim and Emma withdrew to the edge of the front property. Jim whistled.

"All right. Come out now, Tricia. Come, Lola. Car ride."

The two women shielded Tricia into the

car's back seat. Lola jumped in behind her.

"Do what Uncle Jim and Auntie Maddie tell you to, all right, dear? Daddy and I will call you soon," Nancy assured her daughter.

"I will, mom."

Emma climbed the steps to the house and waited by the door. Watchful eyes roamed over the street. Her shirt shifted, revealing the MP5 beneath.

Nancy's eyes widened. "Are all of you packing one of those?"

Emma's answer was brief and to the point. "Yes."

The car door slammed shut.

Friday and Lola occupied the front seat with Jim.

Tricia and Maddie laid low in the back.

"You two stay safe," Jim called to Nancy and Emma. "We'll keep Tricia safe. Count on it."

Jim pulled into the street. Tires squealed as he accelerated to the Interstate.

Nancy moved to watch the car as it proceeded down the street and disappeared.

Emma pulled her past the door and into the house.

"You'll be safer in your home, Nancy."

Emma closed the door and locked it behind her.

Chapter 32

Detective **Boyle answered the** radio call on his Rover, thinking it would be about the crime scene. Often, higher-ups had inquiries. The press wasn't a priority, but when they got a sniff of something, sometimes it paid to dole out answers.

It wasn't to be. The Rover radio call directed him to a second house where there was another homicide. He sent off a second text to Nancy to let her know he wouldn't be home until late afternoon, if at all.

It was a ten-minute drive to the new address. The sun was over the horizon. He flipped the visor to block the glare and put on his sunglasses. He recognized a small park he and Nancy often took Tricia when she was younger. He thought it might be a good place to do some training with Lola—if the crowd was right. He made a mental note before crossing the bridge over the Biscayne Waterway to arrive at his fresh crime scene.

After signing in he repeated the boots and gloves procedure and made his way past a gate.

His eyes roamed the yard. An officer

directed him to the back of the house and the bedrooms. The bodies were in one room.

He scanned the bodies and left to give the examiner time to do her job.

He walked each room of the house.

Downstairs, by the sliding glass doors onto the back yard, another body lay on its back. Two large-caliber entrance holes in the forehead looked to have done this one in.

He stepped delicately around the room, letting his eyes do the work. There was no brass. Whoever it was collected it before leaving. He wondered if it was the same upstairs.

Don turned to go upstairs.

The explosion broke the glass, sending shards everywhere. Broken glass showered the floor.

He cast a quick glance through the doors and recognized a burning yacht. He dialed 911 to call in the fire department and wondered how big of a mess they would make of his crime scene.

He dialed again, and this time made a request for the bomb squad. He made his way upstairs and cleared everyone out of the house.

He was the last to leave.

The yacht continued to burn as they waited for the bomb squad to arrive. The fire department beat them to it, but they couldn't make their way to the waterfront until the property was clear and safe.

It took three hours.

High noon was only a few minutes away.

Chapter 33

Tracking down Luz wasn't easy. Nancy didn't think it would be. Especially given the woman's actions on the day she foiled the robbery. The difficulty forced her to call in a couple of markers from a past life.

Nancy didn't like doing that. She much preferred others owe her.

When she finally found the woman, she grudgingly recognized another professional. She couldn't count the times when she thought she had been made for her efforts. At the end of the week, she knew where the girl worked. She knew where she lived. That was enough. She didn't want to know more than that.

Nancy parked her car in the downtown lot and walked to a bus stop. She checked her watch. If her plan worked, she would cross paths with Luz at the bus stop where the woman got off on her way home. She already knew it was more than a few blocks from where she lived. She would do the same thing if she was checking her six for anyone following.

She recognized the stop. Pulled the cord. The bus halted in front of a busy pub, filled with an after-work younger crowd.

The location was perfect.

L uz liked to assume a standing position well before her bus stop. Today was no different. She kept eyes on a couple of blocks in advance.

She didn't have to pull the cord. There were several in front of her who would exit the bus at her stop. She already had eyes on a woman waiting for the bus. She expected her to get on. When she didn't, she made sure to check her out. There was something—

Luz took a harder look.

Her eyes roamed up and down the woman. Evaluating. Studying. Checking.

No weapons in her hands.

Dark glasses concealed the woman's eyes. A scarf over her head to shade the sun. It hid the woman's face, too.

Luz got off the bus and turned to walk in the direction opposite to which she needed to go.

"You're going the wrong way."

Luz whirled.

Recognized Nancy.

Eyed both hands hanging down at her side.

As if reading her mind, the woman moved to reassure her.

"It's in my handbag, remember?" Nancy reminded her.

Luz relaxed. Not all the way. She stayed tense. Already knew Nancy wasn't one to trifle with. She remained ready to attack if she had to. The woman was taller. Her reach longer. She outweighed her.

If Luz wanted the advantage, she would have to strike first.

"Walk with me, Luz," Nancy said.

Nancy walked a step behind. It made her uncomfortable, but when she slowed to allow Nancy to catch up, she continued to match her, step for step.

Finally, she slowed and stopped in front of a bar.

"Yes, this is better, don't you think? We can face one another."

Nancy remained off to the side, just out of reach. It was hard to tell with the loose-fitting clothes the woman wore. It occurred to Luz that the woman was ready to strike, too.

"What is it, Nancy? Is Tricia all right? Don? You? Are you all right? Do you need anything."

Nancy's face softened, touched by the concern Luz demonstrated for her daughter. "You're right. It is about Tricia. But she's fine. Nothing to be concerned about. She wants you to come on Sunday for dinner. She has something special for you. A surprise."

Surely by then Tricia would be back safely from wherever Jim and Maddie had her secreted.

Nancy's eyes shifted from Luz to the noisy bar and back. A group of patrons were readying to leave.

"I promised her I would find you and invite you," Nancy said. "Consider it done. Please don't disappoint my daughter."

The noisy gathering exited the bar, talking and laughing.

Nancy repositioned herself, allowing the crowd to surround her.

They jostled her as they moved past.

Nancy removed her dark glasses and the scarf.

She turned and became one of the anonymous crowd as it continued down the street. It was as though she was a part of it from the beginning. And she was. She had seen them through the window, getting ready to leave.

Luz hung back. Waited. Finally entered the bar and pretended to look for a friend. It was a good place to have stopped. The busy bar provided cover for her as well as for Nancy. Quite a professional when she wanted to be, that woman. Not sloppy in the slightest.

She would not underestimate Nancy again.

She circled the block. Careful. Thinking.

Would she go on Sunday?

Should she?

Luz took her time making her way to her apartment block and the high-rise that was home. She already decided. Like any good guest, she would arrive late and leave early so as not to wear out her welcome.

She wondered what was so important that

Nancy had taken the time to find her and invite her on behalf of her daughter.

She stopped wondering and circled her block again before finally entering the lobby.

Chapter 34

L**uz woke up exhausted.**
She had spent all of yesterday and most of last night into the early-morning hours surveilling her second target. Still, she found herself nowhere near ready. She hadn't found the spotters and hadn't discovered where the spotters lived. Either there were none, or—what?

There had to be spotters. There had to be. Since her last experience got her found out, that was task number one. Spotters. Where were they, and where was their house? Where were they living?

And most important of all, how would she eliminate them and continue with mission number two to the end?

Ever since Nancy tracked her down to the bus stop, she no longer felt secure. Sure, the woman was no danger. But was that true? If she went to all the trouble to find her, surely others could, too.

Provided they knew who they were looking for, of course.

She tried to be so careful on her first hit in

her new city. She spent months on it. Surveying. Studying. Memorizing. Attack routes. Escape routes. And still she had been spotted.

She was thinking she wasn't as good as she thought she was—although she never truly thought she was that good at the profession that had chosen her.

It wasn't always so. When Luz was first starting out, when she learned she could do what others were doing, she had set her mind to it. Some of them joked about the job. Others talked too much to friends. They didn't seem to be aware of the consequences. And consequences there were. Unrelenting. They disappeared, never to be seen or mentioned again.

Ever.

That was her first lesson. The work is serious. Keep your mouth shut, even to others in the school. Never ever mention it, no matter who asked.

She kept to herself. Tried harder than most. Treated each assignment as though her life depended on it. That wasn't a problem.

She knew her life depended on it.

She fit in well, and caught the eye of one leader in particular.

And here she was, like a rank amateur more than the seasoned professional she was known to be.

Despite having hundreds of kills to her

credit, she felt like a beginner all over again.

It was humbling.

Luz took out the paperwork and spread it over the living room table. It didn't matter. No one was coming to visit. She had no friends. It wasn't like Nancy's place. People in the neighborhood were always coming over for coffee or to gossip or both. Nancy treated them all equally. It was good cover, one that she didn't forget.

She believed Nancy Boyle to be a professional, too. If she ever found herself in a similar position—

Luz shook her head. That would never happen in a million years, and she knew that. She was sure she would be in prison or dead before that happened.

Luz checked her list one more time. She didn't have to. It was out of habit more than anything else.

She had memorized it years ago.

The only addition had been Santiago, at the bottom.

The names of her parents, her brother, and her sister. Even her dog. All printed out in her girlish script when she was only twelve or thirteen. With a dedicated period at the end of each name, as though that was the end.

It would never be the end.

Even when it was over.

Chapter 35

Luz **had two days** before she was due at Nancy's for her daughter, Tricia, and the girl's surprise. She wondered about the surprise, given Nancy had gone to the trouble to locate her. It couldn't have been easy. It only made her think more about what Nancy's background was before she settled into marriage and family life.

In any case, she entered Tricia's surprise into her calendar with an alert and then put it out of her mind. She found she needed the alerts since she became so dedicated to her missions.

One down and five to go. She needed no calendar entry or alert for that.

She didn't have to be at the grocery store for several hours. She changed into cargo shorts and a shirt and headed down to her bicycle. It still looked strange to her that she rode a beater when she had all the money in the world at her disposal. Of course, it didn't look suspicious at night in some areas she found herself when she was doing a recon, so there was that.

She smiled. The sky was filled with

sunshine and blue sky. It was even a little cooler. At the last minute, she remembered her backpack and had to go upstairs to retrieve it. She would get to work on time and change in the staff room.

Out of habit and need, she bicycled past her next victim's residence. Casual. Slow. Taking in the sights like a rider would on a nice day. There was no park to hole up in to do her scouting. That was one reason this exercise was taking so long.

She considered renting a place nearby and immediately discarded the idea. She had already gone out on a limb with the identities for her rented apartment in the high rise. That was enough.

Perhaps if she started going to bars, she could eventually find someone looking for a roommate. She threw that out, too. The area was wealthy. There would be no rooms for rent here.

She continued on her ride until it was time to be at work. She greeted her coworkers and made for the change room. On the way, she passed the produce manager. He had a thing for her from the day she was hired on. She kept her distance, knowing any involvement would only hamper her task list. Still, if he could be used—

She put it out of her mind for now. After the weekend get-together at Nancy's, she would think more about it again.

Her shift went by far too slowly. Some regulars greeted her. Some didn't. She always smiled and hoped she looked genuine. At quitting time, she gratefully wiped the cheerful look off her face before changing into street clothes for the bike ride home.

"Was that you I saw coming out of that new high-rise the other day?"

The question came out of nowhere. She didn't recognize anyone from the store in her neighborhood. She knew, because she made sure to check the bus stops when shifts rolled over and she had the free time. It took her forever, but she felt secure.

Until now.

"The high-rise? What do you mean?" Her brain raced. She pretended to ponder for perhaps a moment too long. "Oh. Right. I was visiting a friend. What were you doing there?"

Luz slowed the buttoning of her blouse while she waited for the response. She hadn't made friends with any of the other store staff. What was the point? She'd be gone, but mostly it was because she could avoid answering questions like this when they inevitably came up.

She put a smile on her face before turning to the questioner. It was an older Mexican woman. Not so old that she would take a flippant answer and ignore her or cluck her lips in disappointment. Was she one of the watchers?"

"I was looking for a job as a cleaner for the extra money. I can't get any more shifts here."

Luz knew her to be a good worker, for she observed her doing her job in produce.

Frida.

That was it.

"I know what you mean," Frida. I could use a little extra cash, too."

What she didn't need was a co-worker in her building. That would blow her cover. She would need to find somewhere else to live.

Luz was on good terms with the managers. She made sure of that. Perhaps she could put in a word for Frida.

"Have you talked to the managers? Perhaps they can give you extra hours."

Frida sighed. "Not really. I thought it would be impossible. I'm older, not like you young chulas with all the looks."

"You're not so bad. Surely you must know," Luz said. "Go and ask right now. Put on a little lip gloss and a smile and see what happens when they can see you in your street clothes. Come on. I'll go with you."

Chapter 36

Luz hoisted her bike onto the rack on the front of the bus and made for the back where she usually sat. It allowed her to monitor the other passengers getting on and off. It also made certain she got a good long look at her destination, the same one where she missed Nancy. If she couldn't even spot Nancy, someone she knew, how could she carry out what she was intent on doing?

Luz was certain now that Nancy was another professional. The only thing she didn't know was what Nancy was professional at. She had her suspicions, of course. She had witnessed the woman in action. That Nancy had discovered her neighborhood and the likelihood of knowing where she lived didn't give her confidence in the abilities and professionalism she worked all these years to acquire.

It was strange to her, given her capabilities and her past performance of her duties. She smiled like a good government employee in her native Mexico upon reading her performance report. If only it were so.

Luz got off with her bike many stops from home. She spent the time riding around the neighborhood to check it out yet again. Still, she had so many questions. Was Frida a spotter? Had they made her?

Luz went through the routines. Checked her six in her mirror. Used storefronts and their reflections. Dismounted suddenly and bought ice cream from a street vendor. Still, there was nothing. No one she could see or make out.

She heaved a sigh of relief until she remembered the man who spotted her while she was on her first assignment. He was good, too.

Was Frida better?

By the time she finished the ice cream, Luz had a solution. Why had it taken so long? She would dedicate herself to following Frida from work to her home over the next days.

Chapter 37

Nancy **and daughter Tricia** busied themselves with the arrangements for the barbecue. They shooed Don away to commiserate with Jim and Maddie over the fuss his wife and daughter were making. Jim understood perfectly.

"Are you going to let wifey fire up the grill and do the cooking, too?" Jim asked.

Don sighed and Maddie chuckled. "I swear, you two, you're behaving like a couple of teenagers who learned they wouldn't be allowed to go to a party where all the good-looking people hang out."

Friday snorted, and Jim chastised the dog. "Friday, you're with us, or you're against us. What's it going to be?"

Friday ambled over to Maddie's side of the living room.

"You guys. Even Friday knows better than to whine and snivel over a little Sunday barbecue. Come on, Friday. We're going for a run and then ice cream."

Friday wasn't a dumb dog. He recognized the sound of ice cream, two words he had heard many times before. Immediately he was up and scampering to the door.

"We'll see you guys later at the barbecue. If you're good boys, we just might bring you some i-c-e-c-r-e-a-m." She spelled out the words for the benefit of Friday. She didn't want him running off in his excitement.

"You see what I have to put up with on a daily basis, Boyle?"

Jim didn't get any sympathy from Don. "You're lucky, Nash. I have two women and a dog. I can't feel your pain."

"It's a good thing Maddie didn't hear you say that, Don. We'd both be in trouble."

Maddie called out on her way downstairs. "I heard that anyway, gentlemen."

"That woman," Jim complained. "I can't put anything over on her. Come on, Don. Let's get a move-on. I don't want to miss out on anything Nance and Trish have planned."

Lola greeted Jim in the back yard. She behaved like he was a long-lost friend. Which he was, considering he had been first to adopt her. "Lola. What's up? Have you missed me? I missed you, too, you know."

The pair made for the back yard where Jim tossed Lola's tennis ball which she retrieved instantly. She dropped it at his feet for another round of the same. When both had enough, the pair made for the shade of the old tree. Lola sat down beside Jim and leaned against him. Her tail swept the grass.

Maddie arrived with the promised ice cream for later.

Friday sniffed and snuffed and scampered around the house on the search for his bestie, Lola.

"Lola isn't here, Friday. She's outside."

Maddie opened the screen door, and Friday scampered out to greet everyone. He ran from person to person, circling and sniffing like it was old home week. Suddenly, he halted.

"Oh-oh. Friday just spotted Jim and Lola hanging out under the tree. And there he goes."

Friday didn't scamper. He ran full-tilt boogie to the tree and skidded to a halt. He bumped into Lola.

She didn't budge.

He tried to push his muzzle between the pair. When that didn't work, he tried shoulder butting his way between Jim and Lola.

Lola still wouldn't budge.

Confused, Friday sat down and looked back at everyone.

Tricia called the dog's name. He ignored her and barked.

"I better go make peace with Friday," the girl announced. "I think he's jealous of Lola."

Friday tried one more time to nose his way between Jim and Lola. He had no success. Neither was giving up their space. He plopped down again, this time on his tummy, and whined.

Tricia made her way to the pair. She sat

next to Lola, making sure to leave enough room for Friday.

He woofed and got up and sat down between them.

Tricia's arms stretched to circle both dogs.

Jim did the same.

Satisfied, Friday settled in and leaned against Tricia, almost bowling her over.

"These dogs are trouble, the pair of them, aren't they, Uncle Jim?" Tricia asked.

Uncle Jim agreed. "Who would have thought Friday would be jealous?"

Luz arrived and dropped off a tray of goodies for the fridge before heading outside. She called to Tricia and waved. "Manita. Cómo estás?"

Tricia turned at the familiar voice. "Bueno, Luz. Y tu? How are you?"

"You've been learning Spanish."

The girl blushed. "Mom is helping me. I'm not very good yet."

"It will come. We will practice together. I brought some things for the barbecue. They're in the fridge."

Tricia got up.

Friday didn't budge. He was intent on holding out against Lola, who was still hogging Jim all to herself.

Finally, the dog got smart and skipped to the other side of Jim and was greeted with the man's outstretched arm. The dog woofed and settled in against him.

"Spoiled man and spoiled dogs. What's a girl to do, Tricia?"

Tricia looked up at Luz and grinned. "I know. Come with me. I have something to show you. It's a surprise."

Tricia led Luz into the house and up to her bedroom, where she pulled a gift-wrapped box from beneath her bed. "This is for you." She held it out, shy, not knowing how Luz would take the surprise.

"Oh my goodness. What is it? Can I open it now? I don't get many presents."

Nancy made her way upstairs and hesitated in the doorway to Tricia's room. It was plain to see her daughter was delighted by Luz's reaction.

Lola took that opportunity to scamper into the house. With nose to floor, she followed a scent she recognized up the stairs to the familiar bedroom. She woofed to announce her arrival.

"We're all here now. I guess it's time to open it, right Lola?"

Luz scratched at the dog's ears and Lola settled in beside her.

Tricia beamed as Luz unwrapped the box.

"It's my dress!" Luz exclaimed. "I thought I thought—"

"My mom took it to someone she knows to fix it. It took forever, but I think they were able to do a pretty good job."

"They did an amazing job." Luz held up the dress in front of the mirror. "It's perfect. It's perfect."

"They weren't able to fix one tiny piece. I sewed it on with my mom's help. You can't see it. It's on the inside. Right over where your heart is, Luz." The girl reached for the dress.

Luz allowed Tricia to take the dress. The girl opened the top and showed her the piece she had sewn in place. "I didn't do as good as the expert."

Luz's eyes filled with tears. "Oh yes, you did, manita. You did a perfect job. This is the best part of the dress. The very best part. That is a piece of my sister's dress. She was wearing it when, when—" Luz wiped at the tears running down her face. "I'm going to put it on right now," she announced.

Tricia looked at her mom. Nancy smiled back at her daughter. "Then we're going downstairs to wait for you, okay?" Tricia took her mother's hand, and the pair descended the stairs.

"We did good, didn't we, mom?" she asked.

"Yes, dear. You did good."

Chapter 38

Luz **didn't know what** to make of it. On the one hand, she was happy to have the dress back. There was no doubt about that. On the other, she was finding it more difficult to make plans for her next hit, and she couldn't permit that. She had to get on with it, get on with life, with her life. Her life wasn't anything like that of Nancy and Tricia. Or Jim and Maddie. She was on her own. She wouldn't allow herself to think about anything else until her job was complete.

It was the promise she made all those years ago. It was taking on a life of its own. And she was all right with that.

Perhaps that was the problem. She was looking at it as though it was a job. Perhaps it was. After all, she treated it like one, and not like her grocery store job.

She dedicated herself to it like she had a fever. No more would she tell herself it was enough. She had to do better. Do more. Investigate harder.

She had revenge to plot. She had no time for anything but to work that into her life, hour after hour, day after day.

Until she was done.

If she would ever be done.

"Tricia. Is it all right if I keep my dress in your closet?"

"Wait till I ask my mom, okay?"

Luz waited patiently in the kitchen. She busied herself tidying up. Rattling dishes brought out the usual suspects to grumble and complain. Don especially liked to pretend, but she knew better by the way he treated his wife and his daughter. They were number one on his list.

Jim was the same. He liked to make her think he was a tough guy—and he was, as witnessed by his performance on the Cabo wharf and the fast-boat to Todos—but she knew he would do anything for his partner, Maddie. And that included dishes.

She took the good-natured complaining in stride and allowed the men to think she was the weak female. It was all in fun, anyway. It was the family fun she missed so much over the years.

"You gabachos know you don't fool me, comprende?"

Jim nudged Don. "I don't know how good your Spanish slang is, but Luz just called us a couple of, how shall I put it politely—"

"No need, Nash. I'm familiar with the term. Just keep washing and I'll keep drying. There's no sense having the woman think we're not what she claims."

That brought a laugh from Luz, and she

dried her hands and went in search of Tricia. "Well, manita, what did your mother say? Can I keep my dress in your closet?"

"Oh yes. She gave me a special bag to protect it. Come and I'll show you."

Luz was completely taken aback. The bag was special, meant for long-term storage, with dehumidifier pockets and racks for shoes and just about everything else."

"I'm going to need to bring over more to fill that up, Tricia."

Lola and Friday scampered into the bedroom, wanting to know what their two besties were up to. They sniffed and snuffled and nosed their way between the two females and generally got in the way.

"They are such a jealous pair. Lola. Friday. Isn't someone calling for you downstairs?"

The dogs halted for an instant before continuing with their antics.

"I guess not by the look of it, Tricia. Their ears didn't even perk up. It seems they can tell those things all by themselves."

Luz hung the dress in Tricia's closet and closed the door.

Satisfied, the dogs chased after the two on their way downstairs.

Chapter 39

Luz was alone. **There** was nothing she could do about that at this stage of her planning. She built that into it. Sure, there was someone at the market interested in her. She was interested in him, too, for he seemed kind and caring and generous. But she just couldn't do it. She couldn't bring herself to jeopardize her plan.

She would have her revenge on those who murdered her family in cold blood. She would sacrifice everything to get that revenge. She was too far along. There were no consequences so far. That alone left her feeling good about the rest of her list.

Just to be sure, she pulled it out. She didn't have to. She had memorized it by heart so long ago she forgot. Already the list was down by two families. There were two more to go, at the very least. She didn't consider she might not finish what she had set out to do. In her mind, she was well on her way to finishing in record time.

It didn't always have to be this way.

She was a little girl when she finally came out of hiding and took her troubles to the local police. They only shrugged their shoulders and told her she was too young to concern herself with such things.

How did that even work? Too young to report your mother and father and little sister and brother killed by the cartels? She knew, despite her young age and everything her papi had told her, there would be no satisfaction with the locals.

She persevered and went to knock on the mayor's office door. Attendants shooed her out with not even a question as to why she was there.

She knew enough to go to a local paper. They were too frightened to even talk about what happened to her family.

When she got a little older, she wrote letters to state and federal politicians. Their hands were tied, apparently, because the killings were too far in the past and there was no one left who was knowledgeable about taking on the investigation.

They left her with only one thing.

Revenge.

She would seek it all by herself.

She kept her eyes and ears open.

She learned through stealth who to look for in the streets. The watchers. The spies. The liars. The cartel women. The cartel wannabes. It didn't take her long before she knew of them all.

She would put her knowledge to work until she could take up her promise with a vengeance.

She never once thought about having to

live with the consequences of her actions. Why would she? She had nothing to live for without a family. Without family, she was nothing.

They would pay for turning her into nothing.

She would never forget.

She would never forgive.

Chapter 40

Luz **could have walked** away. Could have remained in Mexico. Could have continued to work for the cartels. She was a renowned sicario, after all. So renowned that no one was known to feminize the word when they described her. She killed all they ordered her to kill, with no exceptions. Once the order was issued, there was no stopping her. No calling her back. They knew her for giving no quarter, no matter who or what or when.

She made that plain the first time a cartel jefe called her in a panic. He wanted a hit called off. Canceled. She went to the man who was scheduled to be killed and explained what happened. He immediately offered double her fee to set her loose on the persons who ordered his hit.

She killed both sides—all of them—like it was business as usual. No one questioned her after that. No one attempted to call her off. No one tried to cancel her hits. She was a dedicated professional, unlike most others who were merely street thugs and indiscriminate killers, many of them incapable of doing the thinking and the preparation needed for their assignments.

In fact, when those same street thugs went in for a hit, it was usually behind a wall of flying lead that would cause indiscriminate killing.

Not so with her. She produced results that were exact, clean, and just about impossible to trace.

She got that way by starting young, of course. How could she not? She made sure she got educated along the way. Once she established herself, she insisted on being paid well for her abilities and her services.

Of course, she bedded some of the cartel leaders who became infatuated with her. Still, she refused to think of herself as a buchòn, a girlfriend to a narco gangster. Almost all of las buchonas she knew ended up hooked on drugs, dead, or run off to end up dead. There was no escaping once the cartels got their hooks into them.

That life wasn't for her.

Her money added up, thanks to her Santiago and his contribution at the end of the fast-boat trip to Todos Santos. Jim proved grateful to her for getting him and the girl, Anya, out of Cabo safely. She hadn't expected that.

She had no satisfaction from the officials for the murder of her parents and siblings. The useless officials forced her to achieve her own means of satisfaction, any way she could.

As a dedicated, experienced, and professional sicario, she ended up paid well to extract someone else's revenge.

She used many disguises. Wigs. Makeup. Clothes. Shoes. Limps. Handicaps. Canes. Crutches. Young. Old. Whatever she had to do to get close to her subject, she would do. She even became lovers to some of them, using that to get close. The looks on their faces said it all when the pistola came out and the lead flew.

Still, no one really knew her or knew her capabilities. It was all rumor. She liked it that way. Thus, the rumor was that el Lobo was the deadliest of them all. They didn't bother to use the feminine for the name. She was el Lobo. Or just, Lobo.

And then Lobo disappeared.

Chapter 41

Nancy's feeling of unease didn't leave her when the barbecue ended. Don finally twigged to the list of names she showed him. He was moving in on the two multiple murder cases and the reasons for the deaths. His suspicions confirmed they were cartel hits. Murder methods were determined to be identical, notwithstanding the different weapons used. That wasn't unusual. It was expected. It was the pattern of the shots. All identical.

Whether Luz knew it, she was about to be in trouble.

Nancy now understood it was about a vendetta. Luz was determined to eliminate everyone who murdered her family. The names on her list only confirmed it. While there were no last names, there were enough similarities with the first names that it was an obvious given. If she knew it, Don would soon pick up on it, too.

She wondered how many more on Luz's list remained in Miami. Surely, they would get out once word got around. And word was definitely getting out, given the publicity. By now, they would have moved on. Would any go back to Mexico, hoping for better protection by their respective cartel families and leaders? There was really no question, as far as she thought. All of them would.

And Luz would follow, like a bloodhound on a fox hunt.

Or a sicario on an assignment.

A personal assignment.

Nancy's text to Jim requested a meeting. He responded instantly, as she knew he would. When he showed, he slid a burn phone across the table.

"Two numbers. Mine and Maddie's. Now what's going on? Is Tricia safe? Does Don know what's been happening with those hits?" He was pretty certain he knew what Luz was up to. He realized Nancy knew, too.

"I want Maddie to take Tricia to your safe house. You know the one."

Jim didn't hesitate. "Consider it done. Next?"

"I want to borrow your car."

He knew why. "If you borrow my car, you borrow me. I go with it. You're bent on crossing la línea. You also know it's la línea fina you'll be crossing, right?"

Nancy would be crossing a fine line, and he meant it in more ways than one. Even so, he would help her do what needed to be done.

"Luz is over there by herself. With no

backup. No one to depend on. Only her wits. I don't care how much experience she has, Jim. She needs help. Maybe not for the mission she's dedicated herself to. She'll need help to cross la frontera when she's ready to come home. To our home."

Jim sent off a text to his partner. His phone pinged a response minutes later. "Maddie says yes. She'll be in with Emma and the Jeep. Are you going to let Don know?"

"I already have. He asked me to keep him out of it until we're back home. I'm good with that."

It wasn't so straightforward as Nancy made it sound. Don was dead set against it from the very beginning. He only agreed when he realized his wife couldn't be talked out of it.

"All righty then, Nance. It looks like we have us a convoy." He grinned across the table at her. "Mads is bringing the goodies. The Packard has room for storage. We'll need something for you to drive across."

"I'll walk," Nancy told him.

"You sure that's what you want to do?"

"Yes. I'm sure."

He stood up. "Give me a minute. I'll be right back." Jim returned with a map of Matamoros. He spread it on the restaurant's four-top. "Show me where we'll be meeting."

Nancy marked the location of two cafés. Jim folded the map and tucked in his pocket. "There's one more thing, Nancy my friend."

She looked across at him. "What's that?"

"You need to know I'm KOS over there."

"Kill on sight. I know that, James." She sighed. "When we're done, I might be, too."

Chapter 42

Maddie **and Emma showed** up at Nancy's with body armor for Tricia. "Just in case," she said.

She loaded the HKs into the Packard's compartments complete with four rails. Jim's pistol and the extended mags went with them.

"Nash, if you get pulled over for an inspection, you're going to be in big trouble," Maddie said.

"Nag, nag, nag."

There was no smile on Maddie's face. "Very funny. I'm not coming down there to bail you two out. Emma and I have our own job to do. We'll find a new man to pretend to be the boss of the biz, right, Emma?"

Emma knew better than to touch that one. She busied herself with getting Friday and Lola into the back of the Jeep, where they waited anxiously for Tricia and the other females.

"Do you have everything you need, dear?" Maddie asked.

"I baked cookies for the road trip, Auntie Maddie. I made some for Uncle Jim for his trip with mom, too."

"That's my girl. Always thinking up ways to keep us happy."

Don followed Maddie and Emma on their way to the Packard. "Did you get the HK from our bed?"

Maddie's eyes widened, along with Emma's. "You know about that?"

"Not until I wondered why my side of our new bed was so uncomfortable. I left it alone until Nancy moved it to her side. I almost called to complain until I saw what was causing it."

"We left you a little something."

"Jim's spare by any chance? Yes. And two magazines along for the ride."

Don shook his head. "If I get forced into early retirement, you'll find me in the closest mall. I'll be working a security gig for sure."

"Nah. You can come work for us. We'll give you the divorce cases we don't handle."

"Thanks for nothing. Now get out of here before I change my mind and start questioning Emma and Friday about that armored van those two set on fire."

Jim called the group together in the kitchen. "This is your last chance, favorite women of mine. Who's backing out?" He didn't give a one of them an opportunity to reply. "Nobody? Fine. Let's roll."

Don wasn't entirely happy with his wife's decision to chase after Luz. Perhaps chase wasn't the right word. Rescue? He hoped it didn't come to that. "Nancy. Word."

Nancy looked at Maddie. She was no help.

Emma turned away. She would be no help, either. "Jim?"

"He's talking to you, Nancy. I'd go with that."

Nancy pulled Don away and sat down at the kitchen table. She looked around, not wanting her eyes to meet those of her husband. "This kitchen needs a reno, dear. When I get back—"

"It's not going to work, wife. You know—"

"Luz is a part of the family now," she interrupted. "Our family. If I can do something to help her—"

"You haven't done enough already?" Don knew it was hopeless. He went on anyway. "Look. I know you have a past somewhere out there. I know you used it to help get Luz settled. I even know you tracked her down after she moved out. If you hadn't, she wouldn't have showed up for the barbecue."

Nancy considered a Yes, dear, but thought better of it. "I have to do what I have to do. Tricia will be safe with Maddie and Emma. You can count on them."

He knew. Don had witnessed the women in action more than once.

"You can't jeopardize your job. We both know that. What else can I do? Leave Luz all alone out there?" She gestured with an arm.

He realized it was hopeless. "Stay safe. I trust Nash to take care of you."

They stood up, and he hugged her. "And I trust you to take care of my fishing buddy. Who else is brave enough to go fishing in a grocery store and bring it home for you to cook, all while pretending we actually caught it?"

"I know all about it, Don. I'm your wife, remember?"

They walked to the door, chuckling.

Tricia and the two dogs looked out the side windows of the Jeep.

Don waved to her. "Call me when you get there, okay Tricia?"

"I will, Daddy. I promise. Bye." She waved back.

Nancy wanted to reassure her husband, but she couldn't find the words. "We'll be back soon."

Or not at all.

Chapter 43

Luz cursed silently. The last thing she needed was to be back in Mexico. It was home to all of her heartache. All of her troubles. All of her bad memories. Still, it couldn't be avoided.

She had promises to keep, even if they were only to herself and her family, dead at the hands of the cartels.

Do or die, she told herself, again and again. It was looking like the dying would be along shortly. She screwed up. Big time. Someone was monitoring her for sure. Was it the grocery store clerk? Frida? Had she somehow missed that the first time?

Here she was after crossing la frontera. Captured. With no clue where she was being held. Who was holding her. State police? Local? The military? It was probably all three, if she knew anything.

She could hear the back-slapping in the next room. The crowing about how easy it was to do. Heard them talking about Lobo and what a pussy she turned out to be after all. The beer bottles hissed in celebration as they were cracked open and guzzled.

Come to think of it, she wouldn't mind a beer, too. It would allow her to think more clearly. Make her feel like she was part of their plan.

That's it. Keep it up. Soon enough you'll be too drunk to notice.

She worked at the zip ties securing her wrists to the heavy wooden chair. Bent to chew at them. Left plenty of saliva in order to work a wrist free. It wouldn't matter which one.

When word got out Lobo had crossed the border, it wasn't long before Mexican authorities realized they couldn't keep anyone safe. They knew her reputation. Knew they had a real professional on the job. One that wouldn't stop. One they couldn't stop. No matter what.

This woman was no street sicario who used a wall of lead to do her job. Not one who retreated to the street with thug friends to collect the five-hundred peso reward and brag about it. Not one to spend it guzzling cheap booze and using cheaper women.

Numbers were called and deleted. Burn phones ran low on battery and were replaced with new burn phones. Calls were made to trusted compadres.

Nada. Nothing. And they were worried. Who would be next?

They found out soon enough, and Luz scratched more names off her list.

It came at a price.

The trap was perfect.

The trap came at a price, too, allowing Luz to strike off even more names.

She fought hard.

Ran out of ammunition.

Switched to her knives and lashed out so often and so powerful that they dulled. Eventually, she was forced to toss them aside as useless. They found their mark against unprotected skin and flesh. She scored even more bodies.

That move proved to be her downfall. With nothing left to fight with but hands and knees and feet, Luz was overwhelmed. Her last memory was the black bag pulled over her head.

Her assumption was that instructions were to take her alive.

That definitely wasn't good.

She hoped she might find a long-forgotten ally before being turned into a punching bag. Or worse, hung, headless to rot from an overpass.

Someone pulled the bag off. Luz groaned and opened her eyes. She was forced to blink until she became accustomed to the light. Narrow, barred windows open to the weather let in only enough light for her to tell she was in a concrete cell.

Two buckets sat in a corner. They looked new. She expected she was in for the long haul. There was nothing she could do with bound hands and feet. Her knives were gone, discarded in the last fight for her life.

Three knives. Three bodies.

Mentally, she went through her list. Revenge for losing her dog was to be next. She smiled, remembering the first time she saw Anya with her puppy, sweet little Cosa. Anya had called her Oreo because her dog was all black and white fur.

Well, dog or no, she was in for it now. How long would it take them? Would they let her sit and stew for a while, with no food and water? For how long?

She wriggled her hands. The wrist straps weren't so tight that she couldn't regain some circulation. They must have run out of them, because her ankles were wrapped in duct tape.

If only she had kept one knife—

Tricia would be left with her dress. She wondered how long the girl would keep it. It wasn't something someone who wasn't Mexican would wear. It was too frilly and had too many beads and reflectors for an American girl.

Lola was a poor replacement for Cosa. She was just a big, dumb yellow Labrador. They bonded, and she enjoyed sitting on the grass beneath the backyard tree with the dog. She smiled, remembering how jealous of them Friday was. He wanted to weasel his way between the threesome of Santiago and Lola and Tricia. Friday had finally gone on the other side of Jim to get the familiar pets and scratches.

Luz woke up with a shiver. She tested her hands, first one, then the other. Still bound. Hands and feet numb. She looked around to the open door to observe two men. That had to be what disturbed her unholy sleep. They didn't look Mexican.

She must have passed out again.

The next time she opened her eyes, the men were gone.

Chapter 44

Jim Nash checked the two cafés regularly where he was supposed to meet up with Nancy Boyle. They were on the east side of Matamoros, on Highway 2. He remembered the highway from his Baja adventure, and was surprised to learn it crossed the top of Mexico from east to west.

Naranju and Caranju. The two coffee shops Nancy showed him on the map. Orange and Carnation. Caranju was all by itself on an isolated part of the highway, and he wondered if that was why Nancy chose it. The other, Naranju, was closer to town, busier, and frequented by some shady looking characters, to say the least.

There were plenty of young lookouts—kids more like it—in front and in back of the Naranju. He wasn't surprised, given how Nancy had talked about them.

He liked the Caranju. Plenty of open space and nothing to get in the way if they had to depart in a hurry. It was obvious why the cartels liked the outskirts, too, probably for the same reason. Strangers were easier to spot. The sight lines were better. And there would be no doubt about who you might have to shoot.

His car was a standout, though. The old Packard could be spotted a mile away, and no doubt it was being talked about. Ideally, he'd like a place to park it where it would be ready if needed.

He was wondering about that when Nancy walked into the café with backpack and boots. She was dressed almost as Luz had been when she walked into the diner in Largo.

He didn't get up.

"Did you have any trouble, James?"

The old Packard was loaded with firearms for both of them. A small armory, if truth be known.

Nancy had walked across la línea. He looked out across the lot and spotted the old vocho, the Volkswagen.

"Not really. I got a green light. The touristas in front took all the heat, and I skinned right on by. I like American tourists. Nice ride you picked up."

"We're going to have to dump the barge, Jim. It stands out too much. We need to find somewhere we can meet up when we head back."

"I've been thinking about that. You seem to know your way around these parts. What have you got for me?"

Nancy waived off the approaching waiter. "Follow me."

Jim left a ten on the table and made for the car. He followed Nancy to an underground parking lot beneath a newer office building not far from the downtown bridge. She pointed to a stall, and he worked the huge Packard into it while she went past. When she returned ten minutes later, he almost didn't realize it was her. She had commandeered another vehicle.

"This place looks like it could be our fortress. Or our tomb."

She nodded. "I guess we'll find out."

He helped Nancy load the firearms into the stolen Ford. "If we need to do an arms deal to get out of this country, we have the goods, Nancy."

"I have you and Maddie and Emma to thank for that. She left me one of those HKs under the bed. Don wanted to send back the mattress until I finally figured it out and moved it to my side."

"Does he know why you're here?"

Nancy didn't look up. "No."

"Are you going to make me drag it out of you? Not that I could, if I know you."

Nancy sighed audibly. "Luz is my daughter."

"Okay then. That's all I need to know." He meant it, too, but she went on, unbidden, using the opportunity to unburden herself.

"It was long before I ever met Don. High school. Young love. I got pregnant. I couldn't keep her. My parents knew a family, and they adopted her. I had no idea she would end up in Mexico. In fact, I didn't know it until she showed up in Largo."

"Does Luz know?"

"No, she doesn't."

"And Don?"

"No. But he will first thing when I get home."

Jim looked across at Nancy. "I don't need to know any more."

She tossed the keys. "Thank you, James. Now let's go get my daughter."

Nancy's burn phone rang. She held up her hand to halt the proceedings.

"Who did you give the number to?" She waved me off and moved away. She returned with a resigned look. She unfolded the map on the Packard's hood and picked up a pen. She ran her finger down the map and circled a block.

"She's here. Concrete building. Block wall five feet high. Glass shards on top. Gated on two sides."

Jim put the top down on the Packard. Nancy gave him a look, and he was forced to explain it was the only thing he would have trouble replacing if it ended up damaged.

"Seems to me that's the least of our worries."

He grinned at her. "Well, like you, I have my priorities, old friend."

"Is there anything I need to know about Luz, James? Anything at all?"

He considered for only a moment. "Yes. Don't get in front of her if she's armed. Nothing will stop her. Nothing. If you try to stop her, she'll kill you."

Nancy didn't tell him she saw the video of

the firefight on the dock in Cabo. Jim was in front of Luz, and she held fire until he moved aside. She wondered if there was anything to that at this stage of the game.

"You two aren't romantic—" she began.

He didn't give her a chance to finish. "Good grief, Nancy. She was a mere child on that wharf. She's only a few years older now. I'm not inclined that way. I prefer my women older. I also prefer them to not be deadly killers unless they're saving my ass, if you get my drift."

Chapter 45

Up **to now, he** and Nancy had never talked about their target. Now that they were together, the conversation could turn to the objective.

"How did you find out where Luz was being held, Nance?"

"I paid a contact at the store where she worked. She followed her home one day after her shift. From there, it was easy. I knew I was taking a chance if Luz found out the woman was tailing her, but I was pretty sure Luz wouldn't harm a complete amateur. I was right."

"So that's why she skipped out on all of us. She was catching up on the names on the list."

"You had that figured, too."

"Once I learned Luz's family was murdered by cartel hit squads, it didn't take long to put two and two together. After witnessing Luz in action on the dock in Cabo, it became plain as day."

Jim said, "Luz came over hell-bent on revenge. I don't blame her. Already she's stroked two off her list. I suspect she learned number three got back across the line to where they think they'll be safer."

If anyone could be safe in Mexico.

"They won't escape Luz over here, if I know how good she is."

"She's good, Jim. Don has no idea she's the one responsible for those Mexican family killings, but I think he's on his way to finding out. Once he does—"

"We'll cross that bridge when we come to it."

Nancy pulled a Matamoros map out of her backpack and opened it. She pointed to two areas already circled. "That's where we're going. If we're lucky, it will be door number one. If we're not—"

I

He slowed and halted at the exit to the office building's parkade. "What are you doing?"

He hit the Home button on the truck's GPS. "If we need to get back here in a hurry, we'll be on autopilot."

"Good idea. I'm glad I brought you."

Nancy might eat those words if news got out he was down Mexico way. Being kill on sight wasn't good news. She would suffer along with him if he knew Mexican cartels. Don wouldn't be a happy camper. Their friendly fishing trips would suffer, too.

Nancy kept the map in her lap and called out directions while Jim did the driving. They worked well together. She gave him plenty of time to get set up for lane changes and street turnoffs.

"Are you this patient with Don?"

She laughed. "Hardly. He needs to know who the boss is, Nash. Tricia and Lola adore him too much."

"Yeah, Lola is a good dog, isn't she? I still regret giving her up, even though I know she has a good home. I wonder if Lola is tired of all those tea parties yet?"

"Tea parties? You need to get over more often, James. Trish has graduated. She's reading Lola and Friday stories now until all three of them fall asleep. I'd show you pictures if I had my phone."

Nancy looked out the window and checked her map.

"You need to turn here and park. We need to do a bit of a stakeout. If you head into the bodega and get us some coffee, I'll be happy."

Nash opened the door and hesitated.

"What do you like for snacks?" He didn't see Nancy as a snack person.

"I'll be getting us some at that taquería over yonder. It'll give me a chance to connect with the neighborhood. You get us the coffee."

"My kind of woman who likes to snack on street food. I'll have shrimp, por favor."

They ate haphazardly as Nancy pointed out the objective, all while keeping an eye on the street people. Young kids were around. He figured they were only pretending not to pay attention to them.

"The vendor says it's not so bad here yet. Not too many kids with prying eyes. She knows about the safe house. She says it's not very busy.

Maybe, maybe not. I'm not sure we can trust her."

"If she's a local, she'll be fed up with the cartel crap, Nancy. They all are. I'll go have a word with my fractured Mexican."

He returned to the truck with two Sol and enough information to satisfy his curiosity. "This is the place. Mamacita says she saw someone—a woman—being led into the place yesterday evening."

"I declare, James. You do have a way with the ladies, don't you? I would have figured her for forty with half a dozen kids."

"Maybe she does. That doesn't mean she doesn't deserve to be treated right. We want her to help us, don't we?"

He moved to open the door.

"Now where are you going, Nash? We have all the beer and food we need—"

"She needs to know to clear out. This could turn into a kill zone real fast."

"Are you sure? Do you trust her that much?"

"I'm sure on both counts."

"In that case, ask her if she's been inside any of the houses on the street. They all look alike."

They waited until dark. There was no concern about street lighting. There wasn't any, not so unusual for these parts. Mamacita was long gone, perhaps taking his advice to clear out. He must have been sleeping when she did.

Jim's head hit the glass and he woke up when Nancy dug into his ribs with an elbow.

"It's go-time, James."

"Cripes, woman. Do all of you spend time sharpening those things or what?"

"Quit complaining, Nash. Maddie should have had you trained up by now. If she doesn't, I need to have a word with her."

He rubbed at his ribs. "Thanks for letting me get some shuteye."

"It's the least I can let a man do." She rolled her eyes and it was all he could to grin.

"Come on, Nance. It's time to arm up."

He spotted Mamacita across the street in the dim light from the closed bodega. "She's over there watching us."

Nancy ignored him and continued preparing to go into the house.

He waved.

Mama waved back with a huge smile to boot.

"Either she's for us, or against us. I can't tell."

The pair made their way toward the house, expecting the worst.

There was nothing.

No lookouts.

No spotters.

No watchers.

They didn't waste time with niceties. No announcement. No pronouncement. He kicked the door in and entered. Nancy entered behind him, like the pro she no doubt was in another life.

"I'm a little rusty, James."

"You're doing just fine, girl. Follow me."

She gripped his shoulder and they advanced from room to room.

Early evidence said there was nothing to be concerned about.

There was nothing but broken furniture.

And dead bodies.

Chapter 46

The damage was all around them. Broken furniture and dead bodies were everywhere.

"Luz was here," he said. "If it wasn't her, it was her twin."

They were in the room where they presumed Luz had been held captive. "Are you sure it was here?"

The hallway to the room was filled with more bodies, forcing them to step over or around them. They took a quick inventory, running through what they thought happened.

"It looks like it started here, in this room. She must have freed an arm and made a grab for a pistol."

He picked up a plastic wrist cuff discarded on the floor. It was broken cleanly. There was blood on it. Bodies lay on top of one another. They were dispatched with a single shot to the head: front, back, or side.

"She advanced out of the room. By then, the hallway must have started to fill with men rushing to get to the room and to her. All of them would want to get credit for the kill," he said.

Immediately he thought back to the dock in Cabo. There was no holding Luz back there, either. Even then, Luz extracted her vengeance the only way she knew how.

Here, it was body after body. She mowed them down like trees in a forest and kept right on going. He pictured her halting only to pick up another weapon before she carried on firing to continue the killing spree.

"When she got to the door, she halted, James. Look."

Nancy pointed out three automatics tossed aside. The magazines were missing. She must have gone back three times.

"She reloaded and then went back. They were all dispatched with a shot to the heart. She didn't want to waste ammunition on her first foray."

Immediately he felt Nancy knew it could be no one but Luz, even if she initially had some doubt. The small patch of material she helped her daughter sew on the inside of Luz's mother's dress over her heart must have told her everything.

"The list of names. They're the people responsible for her family's killing. Luz is hell-bent on revenge, Jim. We're not going to be able to stop her if these guys couldn't."

Hell-bent or not, he was going to try. With or without Nancy. He owed it to Luz to get her home. "You don't have to stay, Nancy. I can do this on my own."

Maybe he could. Maybe he couldn't. It wasn't his first foray into Matamoros, but it very well might be his last.

"No, James. We're in this together, come hell or high water. Luz is going to be the hell. I don't know what the high-water mark will be. Do you have Maddie's phone number handy?"

"It's in your burn phone, remember?" he said.

"Oh, right. The carnage that woman wreaked all by herself shut down my brain for a minute."

Nancy didn't move off when she made the call.

Maddie must have picked up right away, because the conversation went fast and furious from there. He learned Tricia was fine. Friday was good. Lola was being Lola. Maddie said hello.

When she finished, she cleared the numbers and wiped the phone before tossing it aside. He was pretty sure Maddie would do the same.

"All righty then. Let's get going. We're burning up the dark."

"You know you won't be able to call Maddie again. She just tossed her phone into the bay."

"No prob, Jimmy."

It was Anya's pet name for him, and it annoyed the hell out of him.

"We're of like mind."

Nancy must have known, because she grinned.

He drove them toward the second safe

house Nancy had circled on the map. She passed on her directions just like she did the first time, except now, they were in the dark in more ways than one. Had Luz extracted any confessions from her kidnappers? He never bothered to look for signs of torture, and he knew Nancy hadn't, either.

"Do you think Luz beat us to it?"

"I'd hazard a guess and say yes. You're thinking the same."

It was true.

The neighborhood was a little more modern. Some street lighting. No vendors to watch out for us even if we wanted help. It looked to be another quiet one, though. He figured it was loaded with families with plenty of children. Would they be working for the cartels?

"Somehow, I suspect this isn't going to be like the last place, Nancy."

"We won't know till we get there."

He parked the truck and left it unlocked in case they needed a quick getaway. He should have known better.

The front door to the house was open. They walked through with weapons drawn. The carnage was identical. Bodies lay scattered from back of the house to front.

"Look at that. She kicked in the back door and exited through the front."

It was true. The bodies lay in the opposite direction to those we witnessed in the last house but for the rush to the front door there, too.

"That woman scares me, Jim," Nancy admitted.

He couldn't disagree. "She scares me, too, but she's not after us."

"I wouldn't be so sure. Your name was on the bottom of her list. Okay, it wasn't your name. It was Santiago. Don told me Luz called you that when she recognized you in the Largo diner."

He couldn't deny it. He heard the name, too. "I'm KOS down here. Maybe someone gave her a contract, and she chose to do nothing about it."

"Or she hasn't done anything about it, yet."

He put that out of his mind. They had more pressing matters.

"Now what the hell are we going to do, Jim? We're out of options and safe houses."

But they weren't. He suddenly remembered the safe houses he'd scoped out years earlier. "If you can find the neighborhood on that map of yours, I can take us to a couple of others. What do you think?"

"What were you doing down here, Nash? I thought Matamoros was my old stomping ground."

"Well then, Nancy old friend. We have something in common after all these years besides a couple of holes in your kitchen and a refinished floor."

He held up a hand for silence.

Nancy nodded.

He heard it again.

"Lobo. El Lobo está de vuelta. Ha vuelto."

There was a wheeze, and then nothing.

"Did you hear that?"

"Yes. He said Lobo is back. He didn't even use the feminine construct. They think of her as a man."

Jim turned to regard the destruction surrounding them on the floor. He couldn't believe one person—even Luz—could cause it all by herself.

"If she's the Lobo he's referring to, it's going to be hell and high water now, James."

He no longer had any doubt.

This was house number two.

Luz was having her revenge on all of them.

Chapter 47

Jim still had trouble believing Luz could be responsible for such a trail of destruction and death. How could this mere girl that helped him on Baja sur have ended up a cold-blooded killer?

"I've been thinking about that list."

Nancy said, "What about it, James?"

"She did two kills back home. I think you'll agree from the news that the names matched those of the first two on her list, did they not?"

Nancy didn't hesitate. "I agree. Mother and father. Mamaíta and Papaíto. The first two houses stateside."

"The others would have made some quick phone calls and got the hell out as fast as they could when they saw the news."

Nancy thought immediately of Luz's dress and how Tricia had insisted on sewing the tiny patch of material where it would settle against Luz's heart. Had Luz confided in her daughter that the material was all she had left of her sister?

"I need your phone, Jim."

She walked away and called Maddie. It was the only number in the phone. When she returned, she had her answer. "Tricia says the bit of cloth she sewed into the dress was from her sister's dress."

So he was right. "Thus the second shot through the heart."

Nancy didn't say anything. There was no need. She tossed the phone for emphasis. "Now all we have to do is find her."

It was still dark when Nancy guided them to the third safe house. He parked with a good view. Plenty of cars on the street for cover. A minimum of street lighting to make it obvious they were watching. A shadow moved in one of the cars.

"I'm going to take a bit of a walk. I'll be back in a couple," he said.

He let the door drift back without closing it. Whoever was in the car couldn't possibly have spotted him. He made his way toward it in the dark. Could it be?

He heard a click. He recognized a car door unlatching. It didn't open. Someone saw him after all. He wanted Nancy for backup, but he told her to stay in the truck.

Damn my stupidity.

If it was Luz. If she didn't recognize him. If she thought he was a sicario bent on killing her. He would be dead in seconds. He tried not to linger on that last.

A shadow exited the car.

Luz.

Dressed in black.

Feet in shooting position.

She had the HK leveled and aimed in his direction. The muzzle didn't move a hair.

Talk about stupid things that run through a mind when you find a gun is pointed where you don't want it pointed. Was it one of our HKs?

"Santiago. What are you doing here?" Luz asked.

The muzzle stayed steady, reinforcing his belief Luz would kill if someone—anyone—tried to interfere in her business. He thought only one thing. The woman was ready for combat.

"We came to take you home."

"We?"

Nancy chose that moment to approach and show herself on the opposite side of the street.

He thanked his lucky stars. Nancy was in an excellent firing position. It wouldn't matter a whit if Luz intended to pull the trigger. He would be a goner, no matter the outcome. If he knew Luz, Nancy would be, too. He called to her.

"Leave us be."

Nancy retreated immediately, but kept her firing line. Would she be able to move on her daughter if she had to?

"You brought backup. She is good at what she does, too."

"Yes. I know. That's why she's here with me. We came together to bring you home."

Luz didn't consider the option. "I cannot leave. I have more to do."

"No, Luz. You already have your mother and father. Your sister, too," he said.

"Si. Manita. But I have one more before I will be satisfied."

She didn't use the word happy. That was good, at least. "Hermano."

"Si. Hermano."

She said it so quietly and with so much love, he barely heard her.

"And this is the house of los asesinos de mi hermano, Santiago."

Her brother's killers.

Chapter 48

Something was bothering him. Something wasn't right. The count. The kill count. He couldn't put a finger on it, but he knew there was something. Something he wasn't considering.

Nancy agreed to come along to help Luz. He couldn't say no to a woman helping her daughter, could he? Even if the daughter didn't know it. Yet.

He would ask the question later. The question of who Nancy would have pulled the trigger on. If she would have been capable of pulling the trigger on her daughter.

Did he have to know? Would she even tell him?

"All right, you two. We're ready to go. I'll take the back door. You two go through the front. We'll meet in the middle. Are you happy with that? Please don't forget who you're meeting up with once you get there.

Terse nods said the tension was high.

They were ready.

"Count to twenty and I should be at the back unless I fall into a pit."

The door didn't give first kick. Of course not. It was a cartel safe house.

He unleashed a burst from the HK and kicked again. It swung open and slammed into the wall. He fired a three-burst blind at waist level. Screaming and cursing greeted him.

He called it progress.

He went on full automatic and fired a longer burst.

He cleared the kitchen and hesitated at the doorway to the hall. Where the hell were they all coming from?

More firing from front of house told him Nancy and Luz were keeping busy, too.

They met in the living room, and he knew he'd been slacking. The pile of bodies was scary. He had never seen anything like it.

"All right. Let's go, ladies. We need to—where's Luz?"

He turned in time to see her climbing the stairs.

Of course.

The bedrooms would be up there.

Nancy moved to follow.

 called softly to her, not wanting to be alert anyone waiting at the top of the stairs.

"Nancy. No. It's not your business."

She hesitated. Her foot halted on the third step. She turned to look back at him.

"Don't do it. She's finishing it. If you try to stop her, she'll kill you."

She looked up the stairs, realizing what Luz was intent on doing. Gunshots rang out. Two. Followed by two more.

"If she kills you, it leaves me no options," he said. "I'll have to kill her."

Another two gunshots, followed by a pause, and a muffled voice. Then a final two, followed by silence.

Nancy sighed, resolved not to interfere. "Very well."

She replaced her magazine, and they waited.

Luz descended the staircase. She reached us, wiped her handgun, and dropped it. "I am finished," she announced.

Nancy held up her hand. "In that case, I have a plane at the airport south of town."

Jim couldn't believe what he heard. "What?"

She looked at him, trying to apologize without saying anything. He couldn't blame her. If Luz was his child, he knew he'd be doing the same thing. He wouldn't tell a living soul. Since everyone surrounding them was dead—

"If we leave now, we should make it."

He only had one thought. "In that case, call Maddie when you get airborne, will you? Tell her I'll be driving across to pick her up."

What the hell. The Packard was armored. It wouldn't be his first go-round, even if he didn't have a spare driver as backup.

"Can you get us to our parkade, Nancy?"

An HK rack fell to the floor. His assumption was that it was empty. Another clicked into place.

"Of course. Let's go."

He nodded. "You two head back to the truck. I need a minute."

They made the parkade in good time.

Jim made sure to put the top up in the light rain that was falling. He hoped the weather held so the women could make for home. Still, he wondered what kind of setup Nancy had waiting south of town at the airport.

He needn't have. Black SUVs and armed guards met them at the turnoff. Nancy and Luz left him with their weapons—at least, all but one. He saw slip an automatic into her backpack. He was pretty sure Luz had one, too.

His backup burn phone chose that moment to ring. It was Maddie. "Nancy and Luz are on their way to meet up with you, dear."

She sounded annoyed, to say the least. "That's why you're calling?"

He heard male voices in the background.

"Will you guys shut the hell up?" Maddie yelled. "I'm going to finish this call before I let anything happen. Understood?"

The voices quieted.

"What's going on, Mads?"

"There's a bunch of black SUVs in the marina parking lot. Some men in suits want to take Tricia. In case there's any doubt, I am not happy with that turn of events."

"You have an HK aimed at them, don't you?"

"Yes, I do."

Maddie raised her voice. "And it's on full auto." Satisfied she made her point, her voice went back to normal. "Furthermore, these guys don't look like they're happy to be in a Mexican standoff with a woman calling the shots."

"How many SUVs, dear?"

"Three. Does it matter?" she said.

"Yeah, no. They're with Nancy. She wants you to let them take Tricia and Lola to Tyndall to meet up with her. She'll have a private jet waiting to take them all home."

Now Maddie was really annoyed. "What? Tyndall? I'm not letting Tricia and Lola go by themselves. Ain't gonna happen. She's not even packed."

"Then get her packed and on the road, with you or without."

"That will be with. Right, gentlemen?" It wasn't a question. It was more of a command.

Murmuring in the background told me they agreed.

It made him happy.

"Now here are my instructions."

Maddie sighed, and he could almost hear her saying, You're not the boss of me.

"You will not let Tricia board that plane until you see Nancy and Luz. Understand?"

Already Jim could see her deadly glare directed at the men in suits. "I understand. I will not let Tricia out of my sight until I see Nancy and Luz on the tarmac at Tyndall. Understood, gentlemen?"

There was more murmuring. The men must have agreed, because Maddie said goodbye and hung up.

He hugged Nancy and Luz. Told them Maddie had things well in hand and would meet them at Tyndall with Tricia. She would turn her over when she saw her mother on the plane.

He returned to the Packard, and without looking back, backtracked on the 101. A hurried right at the McDonald's put him on the road to la línea.

He could have hugged whoever came up with those green and white road signs. They were standard in Mexico too. With a well-marked route, he was on his way.

People waved and honked encouragement as the old Packard raced past traffic. She didn't budge an inch when he was forced to swerve past slowpokes.

Using L.A. driving technique, his plan was to own the center lane. He passed under a sign overhang announcing a once-familiar ground: Playa Bagdad. Another said Cantinflas. Wasn't he a comedian?

The route to the bridge was to the left. He raced to get into it in front of a semi. At least that would watch his back if he could keep close in front of it. The driver might get pissed off, but he wouldn't have to concern myself with his six.

A car on my right paced me.

He was on Cinco de Mayo. From there, it should be a straight shot to the border. The only good thing about the car was the number of shooters with a window.

He waited, almost too patiently. A handgun came up.

Was that the best they could do?

He reached across with the HK and blind-fired a short burst. The car disappeared in the side mirror. The trucker laid on the horn and he gave him a wave through the back window.

There was one good thing. The bullet holes were on the right side. The border guard wouldn't even notice. He made a mental note to pick up some duct tape when he got across.

I flashed my brake lights to let the trucker know he was going to slow. He veered into the right lane and tossed the weapons out the window. He was pretty certain the Rio Grande had been witness to that more than a time or two.

Bye-bye Mexico. Hello loneliness and the long drive to the Panhandle. He was going to learn how Anya must have felt, minus a body bleeding out in the back.

He slowed to a halt at the border guard station. The sun was out, finally, and he lowered the top.

The border guard took one look at him and another at the car and waved him right through.

My jaw almost tangled in the Packard's oversize steering wheel.

Jim Nash knew one thing for sure.

No matter what happened, he would never cross Nancy.

Chapter 49

J im Nash made good time on the 10 all the way to Panama Cay. When more familiar ground and Pirate Cove came into view, he knew he was home free. He turned into the short driveway and parked in the lot.

Two curious black dogs double-timed it in his direction before he could even step out. They sniffed, snuffled and barked a familiar welcome.

"Uncle Jim. Maddie. It's Uncle Jim."

Lily ran and jumped into his open arms and the dogs jumped and all four of us rolled around on the grass in front of the trailer.

Maddie opened the door and stood there, grinning like a banshee.

"It's good to know someone remembers who you are. I was wondering if you would ever come back to us."

"Did Nancy fill you in?" he asked.

"She did."

"How much did she tell you?"

"Only enough that I'll be grilling you tonight. Now get your ass into the shower, get cleaned up, and get ready for the barbecue on the wharf. Everyone is happy you made it back in one piece."

Lily and the dogs could only hand out so much welcome-home time. The dogs had places to wander off and investigate on their own.

He was left to his own devices, so he picked up Maddie and carried her into the trailer and down the hall to the shower. He didn't see the small crowd of partiers lining up lawn chairs and a wheelbarrow full of ice and beer outside the trailer door.

"What the hell? They're waiting for someone."

"They're waiting for you, silly. Put some clothes on and get out there."

Jim did as Maddie ordered and hemmed and hawed and pretended he was going to give a speech. For his efforts, he got booed and jeered and finally decided enough was enough.

He cracked a beer and joined the crowd.

He grinned across at Maddie and she grinned right back and everything was good again.

He was left to wonder how he would tell her about the 300 thousand in cartel cash he had stashed in the Packard.

On the drive home, he outlined a partial plan. Fifty for Emma, just because she was such a great and reliable help to everyone.

As for the rest, well, he'd let Maddie help him` figure that out.

What's a business partner for, if not a little monkey business?

About the author

Peter Duke is a Canadian author. He resides and writes in a small college town in the Province of Ontario, Canada.

Aviator. Fire pilot. Motorcycle rider. Vagabond. Drifter. Trouble-maker. Jack of all trades and master of none. Peter has been riding and writing about the places he's been and the people he's seen for more than a few years. Some of his writing is factual; some of it isn't. Peter likes to leave it up to the reader to determine the lies that might be the truth.

pxduke.com

peterxduke@gmail.com

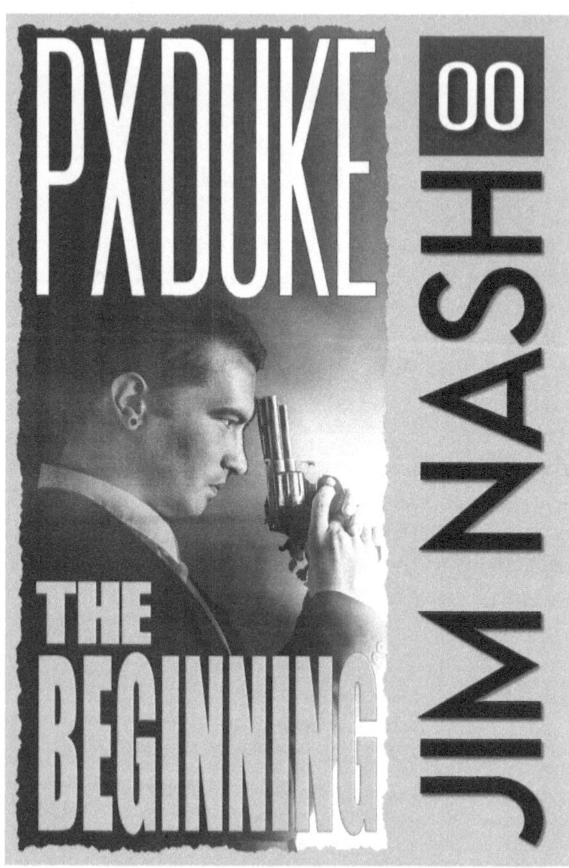

Police Detective Jim Nash has a flawless career in a northern big-city police department until all of a sudden, he doesn't. He proves them all wrong, is re-instated, and stays in only long enough to collect his pension.

Jim Nash Read Order

JIM NASH

Jim Nash The Beginning
Pirate Cay
Thrill Kill Jill
Greetings From Key West
Lost Paradise
No Angels
Mexico Gamble
No Picnic
Fallen Angels
Vendetta
A Girl's Best Friend
Dead End
No Harbor
Dog Days
Startup Blues
Last Stop To Nowhere / The Last Goodbye
Revenge Is Justice
Escape
Wedding Bell Blues
Snap Brim Fedora Caper
Breakdown
Little Girl Lost
Forget Me Not
All The Glitter
Mexico Time
Partners In Crime
Shop Till You Drop
Lobo
No Free Ride
Gone
Stealing America
Blame It on Djibouti
No Escape
Trouble in Paradise
Nash & Delaney Collide

SEASONAL

Trick or Treat
Helping Santa

JIM NASH INVESTIGATES

The Snap Brim Fedora Caper
The Lady in White
The Lady in Yellow

Print books

Jim Nash

Jim Nash The Beginning
Gun Crazy
Gun Crazy 2
Gun Crazy 3
Fallen Angels
Last Stop to Nowhere
Revenge is Justice
Escape / Forget Me Not
Wedding Bell Blues / Breakdown
Mexico Time
No Free Ride / Gone
LOBO
Stealing America
Blame It on Djibouti
No Escape
Trouble in Paradise
Nash & Delaney Collide

Harry Delaney Adventures

Dead Reckoning
Lie Cheat Steal
Uncharted
Go-Around
Sand Storm
Harry Delaney Collection

Frank Ross Biker Tales

No Way Out
Bad Girls
Bank Robber Dames

Other

The Last President

Check out all six books of the Harry Delaney Adventure series. Find out why Harry makes his way from the North African desert to the Mexican Baja. Discover how he ends up having a triumphal return to the deserts of North Africa.

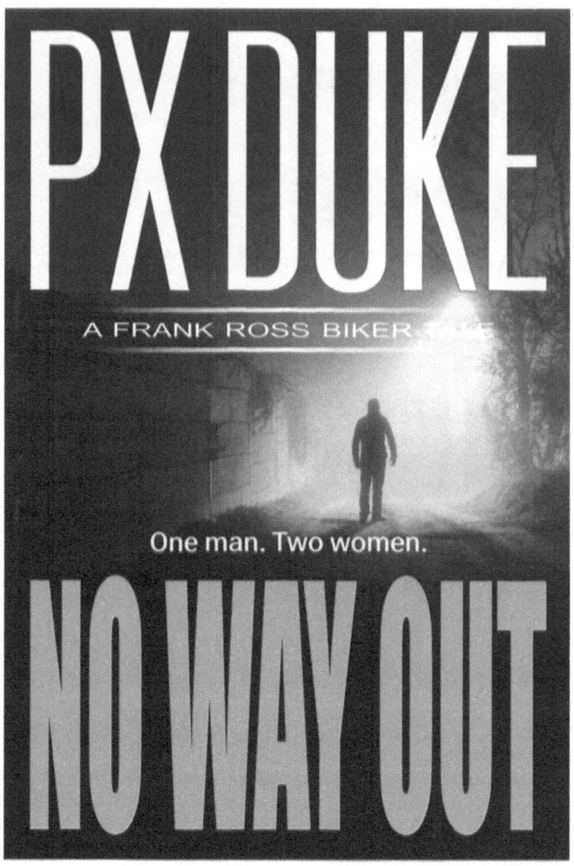

Frank Ross is out of Mexico riding north. He's just across la línea looking for shade and water. He finds it, and a lot more than he bargained for when he breaks down at a casino by the Salton Sea.